Andrew Magnus Fleming

Gleanings of a Tyro Bard

Andrew Magnus Fleming

Gleanings of a Tyro Bard

ISBN/EAN: 9783337327859

Printed in Europe, USA, Canada, Australia, Japan

Cover: Foto ©Andreas Hilbeck / pixelio.de

More available books at **www.hansebooks.com**

GLEANINGS

OF

A TYRO BARD

BY

A. M. FLEMING

AUTHOR OF "CAPTAIN KIDDLE," ETC.

NEW YORK:
JOHN A. BERRY, PUBLISHER
1890.

CONTENTS.

CONTENTS.

CONTENTS.

GOD'S OMNIPRESENCE.

The impetuous torrent in the mountain,
Winds sweeping o'er the arid plain,
Crystal waters in the fountain,
Thunder, lightning, wind, hail and rain,
Attest thy grandeur, O thou Invisible.
Thy glory doth the whole universe fill.

Whether I wander in the dense wood,
To commune with nature in her solitude,
Along the banks of clear, flowing streams,
Or glide o'er the lake's bosom serene,
Through flowery fields, fragrant, fair,
Thou, O God, art everywhere.

To no spot in the universe can I flee
To hide my many sins from thee.
'Mong mountains, in the desert, on the briny waste,
I meet thee, Great Jehovah, face to face.
On earth, in Heaven, in realms of despair,
Behold! O God, thou art everywhere.

BEAUTIFUL CITY.

There's a city built without hands,
Whose glory I long to behold,
And to hear anthems of the bands
As they pass o'er the streets of gold

In this city there's a king
Who sways Love's sceptre over all,
Of His greatness myriads sing,
He is ever worthy to extol.

He was born and lived on earth,
Till we nailed Him to the tree,
He arose to where angels have their berth,
To rule throughout eternity.

The Father and He are on the Throne,
The river of life flows at their feet,
Myriads of angels in heavenly tone,
Souls of the redeemed do greet.

Soon I shall hear their songs,
And behold Jesus, my King,
I will join those holy throngs,
And praise to the Lamb I'll sing.

MY HOUSE.

I will not build my house upon the sand,
For the storm of sin loudly rages,
Before which it would not stand,
But I'll place it upon the Rock of Ages.

Upon that Rock cleft so long ago,
A large and goodly house I'll build;
And when the gales loudly blow,
Behold! 'tis firm as the hills.

Upon its top I will place a brilliant light,
That will throughout the hours of darkness shine;
For many a poor wanderer in Sin's dark night,
Is striving hard salvation's path to find.

Its doors shall e'er be open to all,
And the famishing fed without price:
I shall teach these poor wanderers to extol,
And follow our blessed Master, Christ.

THE FAVOR OF JESUS.

I know I have won the favor of Jesus
And that He calls me His child;
In Him I place my trust;
The world is dark and wild.

Storms may 'round me gather
And lightning break o'er my head;
No power of earth can sever
Me from Him who raiseth the dead.

What matter the few years here below,
Though hard may be our career;
But when to that better land we go
The sun will be shining clear.

On stormy waters we may be tossed
And wrecked on some lone shore;
But He who perished on the cross
Can scatter the clouds that lower.

I know of no other faithful friend
On whom every hour I can rely;
Dear Lord, the time I here spend
Thee alone I will glorify.

A DREAM.

In that season presided o'er by Nox,
Morpheus to my couch came;
His mysterious land he did unlock,
And all within was plain.

While viewing his enchanted land
I beheld a traveller alone,
Clad in strange garb. with staff in hand,
Around his head stars shone.

His radiant countenance made me afraid—
'Twas unlike any of our own sphere—
His voice was like music when heaven's harps are
        played,
And He commanded me not to be in fear.

Said he : "From a distant land I came,
On which ever falls empyrean rays ;
There sin hath left no stain,
And happiness reigns always.

"To earth I came, not for pomp nor power,
Which man deems a glory, though 'tis vain,
But to protect all from the hour
That Satan presents the allurements of his domain.

"In serving me I promise not gold,
Nor few years of pleasure in this world of strife ;
But I do proclaim to every soul
All the glories of eternal life."

When He spake these words
I cried : "O, Lord! all to me is clear ;
From Thy lips the truth I've heard ;
No longer I will grope 'mid sin and fear.

"Long to Thee I were a stranger,
Long against Thee I did war,
And I jeered at the danger
Of rebelling 'gainst Thy just law.

"At Thy feet I bow with contrite heart,
Imploring Thy loving kindness ;
So merciful and great Thou art,
O, cure me of this sinful blindness."

And such was my dream,
The most impressive to me ever given ;
The light that from it gleams
Shall guide me safe to Heaven.

COMPOSED AT A PRAYER MEETING.

In this Temple built with hands
May I, O Lord, worship Thee ;
Instruct me that 1 may understand
How from Thy wrath to flee.

Is Heaven beyond reach
On account of my many sins?
Lead me, O Lord, I beseech,
Show me how Heaven to win !

Long I have strayed from the fold ;
I heard the Shepherd but heeded **not** the call ;
So strong was the world's hold
That I was completely enthralled.

In contrition I humbly bow,
Seeking Thy all-atoning grace :
Ah ! Sin's burden hath left me now,
Onward with the Cross I haste.

The Cross I will ever bear,
Though by the world oft cast down ;
And as reward I shall wear,
Beyond the vale of tears, Life's golden crown.

THROUGH THE PEARLY GATES.

Through the pearly gates I'm sweeping,
Before me lies the heavenly land,
Where the redeemed their reward are reaping
In o'ercoming sins of this mortal strand.

Angels are coming to meet me,
In their hands they hold Life's crown ;
They smile as they greet me.
How their golden harps do sound !

The music is so soft and sweet
That it enraptures my soul,
And in joyance my heart doth beat,—
This joy will ne'er grow old.

The streets are paved with gold,
Such as no earthly prince hath trod;
And O, what splendor I behold
In this eternal city of God.

A SUPPLICATION.

I will praise Thee, Great Jehovah,
Thou hath created everything
So magnificent, Thy goodness ruleth over
The Universe, and in sacred devotion I'll sing
My humble praise.   In glory Thou doth sit;
O, I will praise Thee forever for Thy benefits.

Thou didst bring me forth from the dust
And create within me an immortal soul,
Which now, so vile, doth sincerely trust
In Thy all-atoning Grace.   O, quickly mould
It for an abode in Thy holy kingdom,
Where Thy will by the redeemed is done.

O, show me, great Giver of Light,
Some humble task to perform;
O, wilt Thou scatter these clouds of night
That gather on my soul forlorn;
Just one smile from Thy all-wise countenance
Would prepare me for eternal existence.

All the lusts of the flesh doth stare
At my weary soul, nearly winning it back,
And only Thou alone, most gracious Giver,
Can redeem it from these allurements black;
Unto Thee in humble supplication I cry,
And without Thy favors I shall forever die.

THE CLOSED GATE.

Dear Lord, the Gate that stood ajar
Through which I oft thought of passing,
Is now closed with securely bolted bars,
And it open I can never swing.

The aged keeper hath laid down to rest,
The keys are fallen from his hand,
The sun is low in the West,
Night is gathering o'er the land.

Awaken! good keeper of the gate,
A weary wanderer wishes to enter,
'Mid this gloom he cannot wait,
He has come from afar.

Along the road he came,
He beheld many a wretched soul
Who ignored our Master's name
In contending for gold.

Rise up, good keeper, hear my cry,
The night is cold and drear,
The furious gale that rushes by
Causeth me to quake in fear.

No pillow have I to rest my weary head,—
Jacob found comfort on one of stone.
The cold earth is now my bed,
In pity hear my groans.

Without, I cannot pass the night,
Death is in this icy blast;
In its rage it takes delight.
With gloom the land is o'ercast.

A moment ago I beheld a flame
Within a palace grand and tall;
And voices that from it came,
    rd our Master's name extolled.

This palace is within the walls
That surround this strange city.
O, keeper, hearken to my call;
From danger I must flee.

Alas! good keeper, ye heed me not.
O, my soul! all, all is lost;
Death is thy inglorious lot.
See what procrastination costs!

SAM BANGLES.

Sam Bangles was as jolly a tar
As ever sailed upon the brine;
Into Polar regions he had sailed afar,
And often crossed Earth's central line.

Now, as he had grown old and gray
In sailing so many, many years,
He resolved to pass his remaining days
On land, by salt water near.

He built a pleasant cot upon the beach
On which the tide did play;
His very door the brine would reach,
When storms raged in their fury.

He loved to hear the waves roar;
He loved to gaze o'er the white-capped bay;
He loved to see the seamen soar,
And the storm-petrels on the billows play.

In his cottage he was not at home,
His mind was always on the sea;
That when enraged waves and foam
Would rise high as a lofty promontory.

He built himself a handsome craft,
And to the village he often sailed.
Many a pleasure-seeker laughed
At this capricious tar so hale.

To him the pleasure-seekers were a pest,
They annoyed him with strange questions,
And not a moment could he rest
From those he strove to shun.

Invariably he had a tale,
Such as a tar alone can spin,
And on each occasion he never failed
Attentive listeners to win.

One day a party his craft came to borrow;
Of course he didn't refuse to lend it.
His tattered coat the ladies wished to know
Why he didn't get a spouse to mend it?

At their inquiry he did blush,
And stammer a sort of reply;
Their merriment they could hardly hush,
While on him they directed an eye.

Day after day he was thus tormented,
Which caused his bashfulness to vanish by degrees,
And at length he really wished himself wed,
But knew not how to embark on matrimony's sea.

To instruct him came an ancient maid
Of years outnumbering his own.
Before him the case was laid,
And she pleaded in affluent tone.

Said she:—"You are a sailor, Sam Bangles,
And have sailed long on the salt sea;
Braved the veering gale that came from every angle,
Arousing the waves to their utmost fury.

2

" I shudder at the sight of the waves;
I tremble when rages the storm;
I pray for the seamen brave,
And with their widows I mourn.

" I know of a sea you never have gazed on ;
No sunken reefs environ the shore ;
The beach that many a wave plays on,
With gold is covered o'er.

" There's no need of the light-house,
The hoarse fog-horn never is heard ;
Nor doth the faithful seaman's spouse
Weep on uttering parting words.

"The sky is never obscured with clouds,
And coldness never congeals the brine;
No gales rend sails and shrouds,
But all is perpetual sunshine."

Quoth Sam :—" Ah, that's fine !
Pray tell where it may be ;
I am sure ' tis all moonshine,
Earth contains not such a sea.

" Through Polar regions I have sailed,
Encountered many a field of ice ;
And when strong blew the gale,
We thought 'twould waft us to Paradise.

" In the south sea, 'neath the tropical sun,
I steered my craft good and strong ;
And as she through the brine did run
The wind 'mid the cordage sang a song.

" Perfume on the breeze came from an island ;
Cries of distress came at the same time
From a shattered hull high on land,
'buried in mud and slime.

"Around and in this hull
Lay many a form stiff and stark ;
Some with broken limbs, fractured skulls,
And others with no violent mark.

"This was the wreck of a bark,
Wrecked a day or two before
On the reefs, in the dark.
The waves hurled her high on shore.

"'Mid such a sequestered Paradise
Methought woe far away ;
But often from out clearest skies,
Descend storms of dismay.

"Into no port, my good maid,
That's been my lot to sail.
Have I not heard pleadings for aid,
And the air rent with wails."

"Yes, Sam Bangles, this may all be true,
But you do not comprehend me ;
The sea that I have in view
You gaze at through a glass darkly.

"So, please remove the scales from your eyes,
Which are large as a stove lid's ;
And will you manifest surprise
On being introduced to Cupid?"

"Why ! Cupid was the name of our cook,
Black as night in Hades,
And on a fatal day he took
An accidental bath in the sea.

"The wind blew strong—'twas very dark;
Rain and hail descended fast ;
Poor Cupid, in the jaws of a shark,
Shrieked and breathed his last.

'After Cupid ceased to be
We had many a poor meal.
At length the skipper took dyspepsia
And the ghost he did yield."

" Sam Bangles, indeed you are stupid ;
Certainly you know not what you say.
The god of love is Cupid,
Who to happiness will show you the way.

" Many call me a little daisy,
A lamb, a blue-eyed darling,
But I consider them crazy
Who say I talk like a starling.

" Now, sir, what is your candid opinion :
Am I not meek as a dove,
Or an angel on seraph's pinions,
Soaring away to home above ?

" I possessed admirers by the score ;
Ah ! let me see—that was long ago.
Now, as youth and vanity are o'er
True affection for you I can show."

" Without mistake you are angelic ;
Words to express your loveliness fail.
But do not give me taffy on a stick
While I make ready to snub up sails.

" The rudder I will hard-a-port,
And clew up the main sheet ;
My dear miss, if you wish to court
On the aft hatchway we'll meet.

" S-t-e-a-d-y there, reefs on ahead,
Where breakers dash high ;
Only three fathoms, says the lead,
And on toward the reefs we fly."

"Sam Bangles, you're absurd without doubt,
Your speech is beyond my comprehension ;
Will you please turn your craft about
And bask your old carcass in the sun ?

" I say as I have said before,
That I gaze on a strange sea ;
Old bachelors stroll adown the shore,
Listening to the mermaids' songs on matrimony.

" I know that you in many a clime have been
Banqueted with the Hottentot and African ;
You must have heard the song of the sirens,
Saw their victims' bones bleaching in the sand.

" Have you ever met a maid
That found favor in your eyes?
Your society I'll not further jade,
But leave you alone to soliloquize."

" Don't depart ; your presence I hanker,
And after passing yon whistling buoy
We'll take in sail and drop the anchor,
And drink our grog without alloy.

" 'Tis time we were laconic,
Not whack around the bush like the old Harry,
Or a policeman with his awful stick.
Perhaps, eh ! you desire to marry ? "

" Marry ! O, Sam Bangles ! O, holy saints !
How you astonish me, shock my modesty.
Great mud turtles ! I faint,
And must the cold, hard floor catch me ? "

She fainted, or symptoms gave alarm,
And pitched forward, not on the floor,
But in Sam's strong *arms ;*
Such a burden he had never clasped before.

Within those brawny arms she lay,
Helpless as a stranded wreck in midocean
With helm and rigging all torn away
By the hurricane's impetuous motion.

On her recovery there ensued an awkward scene
The poor old maid was much amazed
And shrieked, " Sam Bangles what does this mean ?
With love or wine are you crazed ?"

" How could I help it?" Sam did stammer,
" On the floor I couldn't see you fall;
If you deem this ill manners
'Tis Cupid's fault, not mine—that's all."

" O my, Sam Bangles, you are noble,
Indeed ! you do possess a heart:
In the future there would be no trouble
If the Fates didn't bear up a part."

" Pshaw ! let the Fates attend to their spinning,
Then there will be no faulty thread ;
The favors of Cupid I must be winning
Or ere long his favors will be dead.

" True as the old ocean laves the shore,
True as the pumpkin grows on the vine ;
Will you be mine forever more?
My withering bud, will you be mine ?"

" Sure as liver oil comes from the cod,
Sure as the ocean is environed by its coasts ;
Sure as in heaven there's a God,
I will be yours till He calls me to give up the ghost."

Nearly every eve across the bay ,
Sam with his boat did sail ;
And ere twilght faded away
He was at the cot of the ancient female.

Till late he tarried with his love
And parted with many an endearing epithet.
They cooed and cooed like Venus' doves
In this most blissful dogwatch ever set.

A month ended this state of affairs,
On a fine Autumn eve they were wed
Then came lambent beams through the air
The honeymoon its sweetest effulgence shed.

From a serene sky it continued to shine,
Not a cloud appeared at the horizon
To warn this harbinger divine
That it could not always shine on.

Month by month it grew brighter,
Like the other moon it did not wane;
Nor did it wax pale when the heavens were full of
    ire,
Threatening thunder, hail and rain.

They continued to greet each other with society
    smiles.
And made use of every parlor air;
No mask had they to cast o'er the wiles
That spring from every-day-life of care?

As the fleeting years passed by
Their happiness was unintegral;
For there were no little ones to laugh or cry
At morn or eve to break the spell.

" Why don't children grow on trees like pears,'
Mused Mrs. Bangles, one eve in June;
As she strolled along the beach for air
In the lambent rays of a full moon.

The tide ebbing smoothly on the beach
In alacrious tones seem to proclaim :
" Your desires are quite out of reach,
But they will be gratified all the same."

Sam cast on the horizon his prophetic eyes
And gave a violent sneeze.
" I would not be at all surprised,"
He remarked, " before morn there weren't rough
      seas."

" Sam, why do you so think,"
Inquired the madame in surprise.
" I can see no clouds the hue of ink;
Like a sea of glass the ocean lies."

" I can smell it, 'tis in the air ;
Had you my nautical lore
You could see it everywhere,
Conspicuous as a barn door."

In the west he pointed out a cloud
Scarcely large as a lady's handkerchief;
Fearlessly over a bright star it plowed,
As when the heavens are storm-miffed.

" O, that's nothing more than a freckle
On the resplendent face of Night ;
'Tis fashionable nowadays to be speckled,
And in fact to look like a fright.

" I think I will cut up my bathing suit
To trim my new hat with,
And on this beach I'll stalk as mute
As the club the baseballer bats with."

" Pshaw ! Cordelia, hold your tongue,"
Sam at length did interpose,
" To nonsense you've always clung ;
I care not what you do with your bathing-clothes.

" You are a silly slave of fashion,
That changes every moon ;
'Tis now my ruling passion
To have a pair of new canvas pantaloons.

" Quite shabby is my sou'wester,
But I will oil it anew,
And my long oilcloth duster
Will last this season through.

" All hands, ahoy! take in sail.   O, fie!
Methought myself on ship's board.
Angry, angry, indeed, looks the sky,
As ever out of which a tempest poured."

They strolled back to their cot;
Sam made ready the rain barrel,
But when upon the eaves he got,
Trying to rig a spout, he did fare ill.

'Neath his weight a cleat gave way,
And he struck in a sitting attitude.
He, being a sailor, 'tis useless to say
His speech was otherwise than rude.

'Twould have been more becoming to a skipper,
In trying to command his crew all shanghaied,
When a broken spar did flip her
Helpless on her side.

" Sam Bangles, hush! I declare,"
The madame called at last,
" The jar broke all my chinaware,
As if in the cupboard there were a blast."

" And what it has broken in me
The Lord knows, I grant.
My first request shall be
Those new linen pants.

" The fright from my fall has turned to **gray**
The greenbacks in my pocket;
My lower jaw has given way;
'Twill take lockjaw to lock it.

" It jarred the filling from my teeth,
Fallen off is every button;
My sou'wester has come to grief,
And so has every dud I've got on."

"Sam, oh, Sam!" the madame called,
"You know of late how proud you've been;
Pride must have a fall,
For it is a cardinal sin.

" I have been looking for it to come,
Ere so late a season.
You are like unto some
Who never heed reason.

"What right had you to seek those eaves,
But one Eve was sought by Adam;
Without asking my leave,
Unto yourself you had 'em.

"When next Eve-seeking you go,
Just heed this lesson :
You are, by far, too old a beau,
Save a cautious suit to press on."

While she her unfortunate Samuel,
Was such good lessons teaching;
'Twould have become her well
Had she taken in the cotton, out a-bleaching.

As Sam remarked : " It was in the air."
So it was : A storm, sudden, terrfiic,
Which began to rage here and there,
With mood uncommonly miffic.

" Those clothes, Sam !   Those clothes !"
Cried the madame, quite frantic,
"Secure them before the wind blows !"
To gather cotton is quite romantic.

Sam began cotton-picking in the gloom.
In this vocation he was quite blind ;
Before him a thousand stars did bloom,
When he brought up 'gainst the clothesline.

'Twas too late !   High in the air the cotton went
Before a gale that gave it wing.
" Alas, Cordelia, we must be content,
As you know, cotton is king."

" Make haste, Sam.   Close is the sea,
Which may engulf every garment.
If such the case should be,
The storm is one of torment."

Each garment was out at sea,
Quite a distance it had got on ;
Sam also went to see
This sea-faring cotton.

Few articles drifted in a bight.
Sam, sad in mind as a mourner,
Ran forth with all his might,
Hoping to create a corner.

'Twas of no use, it sunk short,
The same as it had once been sold.
Sam wished for a long tongue that he might retort
The censure of his scold.

" Sam Bangles, 'tis you I blame
For being so stupid, yet so unique ;
Why did you not tell me it was going to rain.
Inform me, as one should speak."

" That cloud I pointed out,
'Twas plain as prose ;
You could have smelt it, no doubt,
Had you a sea-dog's nose.

I heard it as it careered,
When perhaps two-score miles away;
A person need not be Midas-eared
To hear what Storm-king has to say."

The sea flew before the gale,
Breaking around after both of them.
Mid the uproar there was a sail,
Striving the wild elements to stem.

Exclaimed Sam: "God help those a-board."
The same a thunder-bolt vociferated.
"On the reef she may be gored,
The same as has many a craft ill-fated."

Scarce was the thunderbolt gone
Beyond mortal ears' recall,
When Sam, in tones like a fog-horn,
"Ship-ahoy!" he did bawl.

He seized a single tallow dip,
And she of course her broom.
They groped their way toward the ship,
To save her if possible from her impending doom.

Sam called again: "Ship ahoy!"
'Twas now the madame's season at screaming;
In accent shrill as the blast of a hautboy,
She cried: "Silly tars, of what are you dreaming?"

'Neath his holy sou'wester,
Being far from wholly righteous.
Flickered, as smiles the jester,
The tallow-dip that was thrust.

For several moments it flickered,
Till a sudden gust blew it out;
Like some poor toper over-liquored,
They groped their way about.

Sam at length struck a match,
And held the light between his fingers;
But not a glimpse could he catch,
Of the craft that hard on the reef did linger.

"Ship-a-hoy!" he called for the third time,
And received in response
A faint cry from out upon the brine;
Dolorous as proceeds from ghostly haunts.

Pallid he in tones like Stentor,
Sounding above the thunder;
"The reefs are navigable at the center,
Hard-a-port—don't blunder!"

He was not heeded, if heard at all;
The skipper begun seaward tacking;
It seemed as if they would be enthralled
Within the jaws of death that kept smacking.

At any rate she disappeared from view,
Riding out the storm in safety;
Sam and his spouse, in lieu
Of further gazing, homeward took their way.

On passing a hillock o'er,
They beheld a sight surprising;
The see was knee-deep at the door,
And still kept on rising.

"O Neptune," cried the madam in tones despairing,
Your destructive sport—why, stop it!
Of unwelcome hospitality you're sharing;
Your aqueous feet have ruined my carpet."

At the sea god she shook her broom,
Much animosity she did construe;
"Hateful Neptune, get out this room,
I am desperate, shoo! shoo!"

She set forth sweeping the sea,
The same as did the Invincible Armada;
Toward success she took no degree,
Not a single drop would heed her.

Still she swept, keeping up a constant sweeping,
And, like the unfortunate Danaides,
Her efforts were fruitless; upward creeping
Continued the refluent seas.

"Sam Bangles, you didn't know what you were at,
You possess not the acumen of a carp;
Instead of building on A flat,
Why didn't you build on E sharp?"

" I built before I had intentions,
Of taking unto myself a rib;
Since to my anatomy there's an extension,
It behoves me not to fib.

" Cordelia, let us not quarrel,
Over so trifling an episode;
Let forgetfulness wear the laurels,
That unpleasantness has outgrowed.

" We must be ever ready to compromise,
As Henry Clay was wont to do;
When there appeared in our skies,
Clouds of war-like hue."

While the elements were in their angriest spell,
There came a cry from out the pear tree
That overhung the well.
Frightened they were to high degree.

" O, la me, Sam, did you not hear it? "
The madame on dropping her broom inquired;
" 'Twas something dreadful. I fear it
Is a sea sprite ired."

"I heard it," Sam did reply,
"Pshaw! no cause to be afraid;
'Twas but a siren's cry,
Or that of a mermaid."

Sam put cotton in his ears,
That he might not hear the **song,**
As was sung in olden years,
When the Argo sailed along.

By the waves among the branches it had been cast,
The smiling infant that Sam to his bosom bore;
"Ah, Sam, this will convince you at last,
That children grow on trees like pears, as I said
    before."

TO MINNIE.

Sadly moans the winter gale,
But not sadder than my heart;
This eve at twilight pale
For strange lands I depart.

I would not tarry till spring
To proclaim adieu to all;
Now, while drear winter is **king,**
There is little to extol.

Naught have I worthy of a tear,
But if one should fall for thee,
Deemest thou 'twould appear
That in sorrow I wept o'er thee?

With the past I must be content;
Let the future bring forth whate'er it **will;**
Those joyous moments with thee I spent
Shall never cease my soul to thrill,

Thou wert faithful to thy vows;
But, woe me! I heeded not mine.
My heart must have been weak, I trow,
But why at this late hour repine?

In this last hour I ask to be forgiven,
And I know thou wilt forgive;
Like Him who rules in Heaven,
With the benediction I can live.

From hence depart I must,
Forever barred from the one I adore;
'Tis almost as being in Tartarus
And gazing on that blissful shore.

But wherever I go I fear
Thy fair face I will behold;
Like some heavenly visitant may it appear
To pacify my lonely soul.

In my dreams at night,
When Nature seeks repose,
May thou be the sprite
To mitigate my sorrows.

In some distant sunny land,
Where fragrant is the air,
I'll dance my sereband
And strive to bid adieu to care.

There shall shine my flambeau,
Lit by thy amaranthine smiles,
And through the darkness as I go
My faith will be illumed all the while.

The birds thy beauty wilt carol,
Thy name wilt be murmured by the stream;
Nature in her majesty wilt extol
The one of whom I nocturnal dream.

Endymion like, O, let me not awake,
For " life is but an empty dream."
My retrospective thirst I would not slake
From Lethe's fabulous stream.

Alas! Minnie, 'tis my inglorious lot,
Assigned by inexorable Nemesis,
That I should seek unsought
A most ebon career—as this.

May thy cheek ne'er be suffused with tears,
May thy days be uncumbered with care,
And throughout life's fleeting years
May thou perpetual happiness share.

TO HANNAH JONES.

In my visions by day and dreams by night
There's a being that continually haunts me;
Her hair is red as fire is bright,
And her buttermilk eye sort of daunts me.

O, Hannah! beautiful red-haired Hannah!
Of thee I'll sing in loudest tones,
And in the most sublime manner,
As thou art the only daughter of Deacon Jones.

Ah! ah! thou hast many a lover,
Some young and handsome, others old and thin,
Some tall and short, others lank or plump as a plover,
Some morose, and others that continually grin.

Of the heterogeneous mass I am the most humble,
But thou, dearest, doth deem me the best.
Should thy regards not to dust crumble
What joy will lodge in my breast.

3

There's many a handsomer bird than **you**,
But "fine feathers make fine birds."
If you think this is not true
Go listen to what may be heard.

TO ORPHEUS.

Orpheus, though thy companion be forever gone,
Hang not thy harp on the willow tree;
On the breeze let there be borne,
As in days of yore, thy divine melody.

The loss of whom thou doth sorely grieve,
Would sooner or later have departed;
From Mar's decree there is no reprieve,
Despite the pleadings of the broken-hearted.

Thou did'st love her well,
Into Pluto's domains thou descended;
Braved every woe of hell,
While fiery Phlegethon round thee wended.

She hath gone, forever gone,
Trees, rocks, and beasts, yet list thy lyre's strains;
Alas! never more at early morn,
Noontide or eve wilt, it sound again.

To thee mortal's choicest lyre wert given,
And thou didst attune it well.
When thou and thy spouse meet in Heaven,
There let thy melody forth swell.

TO CHARON.

O Charon! in thy leaky ferry boat,
Clad in that old tattered coat,
Must I like those gone forever,
Pay my passage across the river?

If I possessed Ænæs' piety,
Thou wouldst pass me free ;
No frown on thy face would dwell,
Gloomy as the shades of hell.

If my lyre had the power of Orpheus,
Thou wouldst take me to the realm of the just ;
Alas ! 'tis but one of these later days,
Unattuned to olden time's heroic lays.

Hercules for his valor,
Without compensation his abode saw ;
Since there are no longer bards, heroes, men of piety,
Not a soul wilt thou transport free.

TO FRANKIE.

Frankie, this ring I give thee,
As a pledge of purest love,
Pure as the fount that we
Will gather round above.

Though only a band of gold,
And a tiny glistening stone ;
But it doth mold
Thee, Frankie, as my own.

On thy slender finger it rests,
Like some gem in the sea ;
Glistening like stars that express
Joy in their twinklings of jollity.

Dear ring ! on that finger so slender,
May thou ever be at rest ;
Each season adding to the splendor,
Of the betrothed thou doth manifest.

TO A FRIEND, ON PRESENTING HER WITH A VOLUME OF POEMS.

Many a fickle friend hath forsaken me.
To strew my rugged path with thorns ;
I know I can confide in thee, Jessie,
Thou art too noble to scorn.

Regardless of the distance that intervenes,
Betwixt my place of abode and thine ;
Throughout life's vicissitudinous scenes,
My torch of Friendship will brightly shine.

Always I shall remember thee, as in days of yore,
As a patient, noble, kind-hearted lass ;
Untaught as yet in Deception's lore,
Which causes the most leal friendship to blast.

As a token of thy steadfast friendship,
I present you this poorly written volume;
Which has caused many from Hatred's goblet to sip,
And on me their Satanic wrath fume.

I'm well aware it possesses no merit,
'Twas not intended to be at all sublime;
But it doth the deeds of some ferrit,
Who deemed me too stupid to rhyme.

AN ADDRESS TO AN EAGLE.

Noble bird! Emblem of Columbia;
By alien hands thou hath ne'er been entrapped.
Though often assailed on land and sea,
'Mid the din of battle thou soared enwrapped
With glory. While the stars and stripes
Alone art mate in thy lofty flight.

Where eternal summer gilds the base
Of mounts clad in perpetual snow
Thou wast assailed. And in the face
Of the enemy thou didst look undaunted. Mexico!
Render back the many thousands of our brave,
That in thy virgin soil slumber in a warrior's grave.

At home thou were assaulted. O, shame
To those that banded in rebellion!
Scattering broadcast the candescent flame
Of war. And when the crimson tide began to run,
Each heir to War and Pestilence filed his claim;
Rendering our land a vast burial plain.

Though months and years passed into oblivion
Before Rebel hands relinquished their fiendish grasp;
But all the while, like a Polar sun,
Thy courage flashed, and, quick as the asp
That darts forth, thou smote terror in the hearts
Of all that participated in rebellious parts.

And now, as nations of the earth cease
To gaze on thee with contempt, a single iota
Of courage thou hath not lost. May peace,
Perpetual peace, to thee her homage pay.
Unto thy keeping art given, for all time,
The most glorious land on which the sun ever shines.

TO NATURE.

When Nature in all her majesty is aroused
She shows us how meagre is our power
In her domains. O, man, an hour
May reduce thee to nothingness! Espouse
Not thy greatness, if such thou art. Winds blow,
But thou canst tell whither they come or go.

O, Nature ! teach me thy goodness
And how to obey thee in every iota.
He that rebels doth surely pay
A severe forfeit.   Me, how oft thou hast blest,
And may I never win the low applause
Of disobeying thy ever just laws.

Thou art my inseparable companion—my all.
Thy manifestations did early teach me
To be thoughtful.   What beauty in thee
Is hidden !   The rain and snow that fall
Teem with beauty.   And winds soft or sharp
To me are harmonious as an Æolian harp.

The moon emitting her soft rays
Beautifies the Night.   Stars, the poetry
And song of the firmament, doth say
In their merry twinkling, that Happiness lies
Beyond the pale of this humble sphere,
Where on we grope 'mid doubt and fear.

Northern lights, comets, and meteors,
Excite our wonder, we gaze thereon, and wonder
       much
As to their origin and destiny.   By us, such
Problems are insoluble.   Thy laws,
A mighty code, govern worlds present and those yet
       to come.
We look into, and on trying to read, our lips are
       dumb.

Storms engender; the ocean is lashed to foam ;
When past, it resumes its usual fluctuations,
Bearing onward the ships of nations.
Some, however, are doomed to find a home
At the bottom of the sea, where the leviathan
Toys with wrecks and remains of men.

The lofty mount clad in perpetual snow
Attests thy grandeur. The earthquake, whose rage
Rends asunder the solid earth, is a hastily written
      page
In the great book of Mystery. The active volcano
Belching forth its liquid fire, doth say
That in the bowels of the earth there's no tranquillity

Behold ! daily thou doth create worlds,
And cast others to destruction,—their inhabitants
Are wafted into eternity. At a glance,
From the abyss of space thou doth hurl   [come
New planets, peopled anew. When our turn shalt
Thou wilt waft us far into oblivion.

SWEET HOUR OF EVE.

Sweet hour of eve ! at thy approach
The cares and turmoils of the day cease ;
The weary husbandman reclines on his couch
In comfort. The winds are at peace ;
Gone, art thou, fierce sun-light !
New-born is the rest-imbuing breeze of night.

Sweet hour in which the family circle is united,
The sire reads his evening paper, the mother knits,
The first-born tells his adventures of the day,—
      delighted
Are the younger ones that, with awe, do sit
And listen attentively. The infant sleeps
In its crib, o'er which the moonbeams creep.

Outside this happy circle, cows in the yard
Lazily chew their cud. Calves in the pasture
Are at rest, 'neath the boughs of an oak, whose hard,
Gnarly a trunk affords the woodcock a secure
Nook to hatch and rear in safety its brood.
Up in the branches an owl hoots with impatient mood,

Swine that, throughout the sultry day,
Sought the coolest nook in their sty
Are at sleep.   Little pigs with twisted tails play
Around their ponderous ancestors.   How shy
They are !   They squeal, exerting their vocal throes,
They try to root, but there's a ring in their nose.

Old Dobbin, the carriage horse, is asleep,
With his long neck bent down ;   His nose
Nearly touches the floor.   And, as the moonlight
        creeps
Through the roof, frisky mosquitoes
Begin their jubilee.   He rouses up, shakes an ear,
And wonders why such nuisances come near.

Towser, the huge Newfoundland watchdog,
Lies with his head and forepaws outside his kennel
And lolls.   A toper with too much grog
On his stomach is not more restless than he.   Now
        swells
His sonorous bark.   He bounds and grapples
The pantaloons of a wayward boy filching apples.

Brigham Young, the old white gander,
With his numerous flock is squatted on the ground,
And at each unusual noise he doth ponder
Its origin.   He hisses to warn those around
That danger is in alert.   Perchance a fox
Or wolf in the 'jacent foliage stalks.

Beecher, the Plymouth Rock rooster,
Perches upon the highest roost, with head 'neath his
        wing,
Maybe dreaming of the rich garden-bed he intends
        to stir
On the morrow.   Presently he awakes ; loud rings
On the breeze his clarion which is heard
Much further than man's loudest words.

Thomas, the venerable Maltese, noted for his pilgrim
      ages,
Has just returned with three good-sized cats
One black and the others gray. On the edge
Of the kitchen roof they squat. Many are their spats.
Finally, they begin to quarrel and fight in earnest.
The inmates of the house come out, away they haste.

TO NELLIE.

Nellie, after a long separation,
   On this mild Autumn eve
My thoughts to thee I turn ;
   In this retrospective mood I grieve
Not o'er that which we most cherish
Before our enraptured gaze doth perish.

The heart in which we sincerely trust,
   Will suddenly on wings arise
And soar beyond the flight of Pegasus,
   While the heart that we despise,
In whatsoever direction we're bent,
Whether in light, or darkness, is omnipresent.

From me thou didst take thy way,
   Leaving me with a heart to contend,
That in all the world, both sad and gay,
   Solicits not friendship of friends ;
Nor of the anchorite doth it inquire
Why he from the world didst retire.

Not of the philosopher doth it ask
   Why inconstancy dwells in the breast,
That, under the illusion of love, unmasks,
   Lulling the admirer to a fictitious rest,

From which ere long he must awake
In thirst that cannot be slaked.

O ! in those fabulous dreams
   Of the grand bards of old,
Did there flow Lethe's stream,
   A quaff of whose waters cold
Would obliterate from the past
All that causeth our hopes to blast?

Nellie, thou art still fair and young,
   While I have grown aged—
Not in years, but having wrung
   From harsh experience many a thread
Of wisdom, of which a mantle I'll weave
Rendering me invulnerable to the tongue that de-
    ceives.

TO THE SAME, FIVE YEARS LATER.

If my harp has gained a merry chord
   Since years ago I sung you last,
It will, I am positive, well accord
   With that through which I passed.

It has been my fortunate lot to roam,
   Without fixed purpose, through our broad domains,
From morn till the gloam
   I gathered in pleasure's grain.

From where harsh old Atlantic dashes
   When before an easterly gale sent,
To where the tranquil Pacific splashes
   I have pitched my tent.

"My tent," figuratively speaking,
  Was nothing but an empty grip-sack;
And while thus pleasure-seeking
  A coat would have become my back.

All the while I was happy,
  For care had flown away;
If ever I thought of thee
  I was more gay.

Away forever, away, fictitious love,
  Still further away care and strife;
May I live in a tub,
  Like Diogenes, the rest of my life.

TO ELLA.

I miss thee, dear Ella,
Thou art forever gone;
Like the radiance of a shooting star
Thou didst my existence adorn.

Our fondest hopes—alas!
Have all dissolved in tears;
Not a grain in the hour-glass
Of happiness wilt ever appear.

The sun shines as bright,
But his rays seemeth dim;
And the stars by night
No more by angel hands are trimmed.

No more I behold thy face
Of beauty, peace and happiness;
And, gazing on that familiar place,
I see Woe friend making with Distress.

These guests have taken up their abode,
Where in joy we often used to meet;
Briers overrun friendship's road,
They pierce the weary travellers' feet.

No more, O, nevermore,
Can we be what we have been!
The day of love and joy is o'er,
Separation is a canonized denizen.

The zephyr, once so soft and fair,
Now sighs, and ofttimes moans;
As if encumbered with care
That no cessation hath ever known.

Moan, ye zephyrs! roar, ye gales!
'Tis now all the same to me;
I can comprehend thy wails,
They are akin to sorrowing humanity's.

Perchance thy master, Acolus,
No more greets thee with a smile ;
His bosom may teem with distrust,
Deeming ye each an inconstant child.

Notwithstanding this, I will trust ye,
Take wing, and a message bear
To her who hath forsaken me,
Leaving me to feast on despair.

Tell her that for me there's naught left,
But to wander forth and mourn—
Striving in vain to console myself,
That the day of happiness will soon dawn.

TO THE SAME.

So, the time at last has dawned
For you and I to say adieu ;
O. do not think I shall mourn,
There are many others good as you.

" There are as good fish in the sea as ever were
    caught,"
And my hook is baited with fresh bait ;
By harsh experience I have been taught,
That the most choice fish often bite late.

As I o'er life's turbulent sea sail,
In my own Argo-like bark,
I may by good fortune hook a whale ;
If the fates are against me, a shark.

You were the shark that bit my hook
While I was half asleep ;
Ere I could the cause of the commotion book,
You had run the length of the line complete.

With all my might I pulled at the line,
And came well-nigh being drawn into the sea ;
But when I got you on top of the brine,
You made the foam fly like fury.

But, my dear shark, it was of no use,
For the hook had pierced your jaw ;
'Twas as impossible for you to get loose
As to drain the ocean through a straw.

After I landed you safe at my feet.
For a moment you sort of charmed me ;
But I discovered you were full of deceit,
And would sooner or later harm me.

I cast you back into the water again—what a blessing !
And I rejoiced like a felon on breaking jail ;
Surely, you're unworthy of Satan's possessing,
Save only to flirt and to rail

TO BELLE.

Belle, I would not sing you a song,
One that's light and gay;
My heart is sad the day long,
For I'm going far away.

The Fates, those cruel things,
Say that I must depart;
Their decree, how it stings
And nearly breaks my heart.

'Tis not for pleasure I go,
This boon is only with thee;
Everywhere thy presence throws
A mantle of peace and glee.

Glad will be the old gent
When I am far away;
Till midnight will he be content
Beside the gate to stay?

At dusk no more in the lane
Need he be prowling there,
And with uplifted cane
Warn me to beware.

'Neath those shady branches on that mound,
Where we met many a time,
O, what Elysian bliss I found
For this prosaic life too sublime.

Overhead soft winds sighed
Through the verdant boughs.
Alas! how soon they died,
Like our well-intended vows.

When on thy golden tresses
A glittering dewdrop fell,
Methought an angel's caresses,
Fit only for my gentle Belle.

I saw thy mild blue eye
Cast upward at the stars;
'Twas of a lustre that defies
Those daring rays of Mars.

In accent thou didst proclaim
Those few parting words;
Was sweeter than any strain
From Helicon ever heard.

ODE ON LOVE.

O, Love! thou art a dreadful thing!
Ye set our brains a-spinning,
Our tongue some ditty to sing,
And our countenance broadly grinning.

Ye put our hearts in a flutter,
As if we had heart's palpitation,
And our lips to only mutter
Her name, the dearest in creation.

Between leal friends ye create discord
In contending for the fair prize,
Whom thou dost to the victor award,
While the vanquished gets but a pair of black eyes.

Though ye make our evenings pleasantly short
By ushering us in the presence of our fair one,
There perchance to yawn and court,
Till out the east comes the sun.

Fortunate are we if ye do not bring us in contact
With old Towser, the watch dog at the gate,
Or with the old gent, who knows just how to act
In using that boot of his—number twice eight.

Ye make us hoard every dime
To buy her ginger-cakes and candy,
And to make us appear sublime
In those eyes that may deem us a dandy.

At thy request we crop our hair and shave,
Polish our boots till they shine as a mirror,
Don our broadcloth, put on a stand-up collar, and
    rave -
Because it wants to cut off our ears a little nearer.

Ye make us spend lots of cash
In preparing for our wedding;
On us ye frown—then a crash,
And we divide furniture and bedding.

O, ladies! I love thy winsome smiles;
But deem me not at all stupid,
For I am well schooled in thy wiles.
Away! vain, deceiving Cupid.

I should not care to change my sober life,
For long in bachelorhood I've tarried.
O, ye who are soon to take a wife,
'Tis social suicide to get married.

TO AGNES.

Agnes, dear, I love you,
   And I know that you love me,
Just like an Indian does his canoe,
Or the sailor the salt, salt sea.

My heart is large as a frying-pan,
   And with love it gently beats,
Like ocean waves upon the sand,
   When winds are soft and sweet.

The cucumber may decay on the vine
  And the pumpkin rot in the cellar,
But unchangeable is this heart of mine
  For I am your best fellow.

The sun-flower may cease nodding to the breeze,
  And the morning-glory fail to climb the wall,
But thee I shall ever strive to please,
  My dearest duck, my idol.

The fairest flower is oft killed by frost
  Ere its fragrance is given to the air ;
The fondest lover is oft overboard tossed
  When he is wholly unaware.

I weigh just five-and-ninety pounds,
  True as I weigh a single ounce,
And last eve in the park down,
  O what made you give me the grand bounce ?

I seem to feel my very soul
  Spread wings for its mysterious flight
To that city, where the streets are of gold,
  Glittering always in celestial light.

I know I turned deathly pale,
  And my knees together shook,
My voice was lost in a wail,
  My eyes were full of tears,—I couldn't look.

There was a pain in my head,
  It seemed as if it must burst.
A thousand times I wished myself dead,
  The day that I was born I cursed.

A cold shudder crept up my spine,
  Which made my teeth rattle
Like a raw recruit's in line,
  On going into his first battle.

4

My breath came hot and fast,
　　As if trying to catch a train,
That rapidly rumbles past,
　　When there's yet three blocks to gain.

I tried to put my lower limbs in motion,
　　But on the spot they balked;
It may be a foolish notion,
　　They seemed like so much cork.

I tried to take out my handkerchief,
　　Perfumed with your favorite Jockey Club,
But my hand was cold and stiff,
　　My arm seemed a lifeless stub.

The hot tears dried upon my cheek,
　　The blood in my veins congealed;
My lips could no more speak,
　　Than if Death had them sealed.

Such was my horrid plight,
　　In which I almost died,
I yearned then to be a sprite
　　To be ever near thy side.

O, Agnes, what has changed you so?
　　Last Sabbath didn't you vow
You would be mine through rain and snow,
　　Whether I toiled with pen or plow?

The pen is an insignificant thing,
　　And the plow something meaner
He to either of them clings,
　　Will all the time grow leaner.

My vocation would be the law,
　　And besides a great speaker.
Oh, fie! Ambition is but a straw,
　　When broken, makes one meeker.

Ah! with you I yearn to dwell
  In a cottage where willows droop;
Unbroken would be our love spell,
  Though our abode be small as a hen-coop.

What would be the need of the hearth,
  At which the old gray cat dozes;
We could live for aye on mirth,
  'Mid big sunflowers and roses.

No potatoes need we boil,
  No turkey need we kill and stuff;
We could live so free from toil,
  To live on love alone is enough.

Love-ditties we could sing
  Till our tongues would no longer go,
Then I could pick them on the strings
  Of my favorite guitar or banjo.

The sun will shine when it is clear,
  Rain will fall when the sky is o'ercast,
But to us not a cloud would appear,
  For our love would perpetually last.

When winter gales roar
  And all nature seems dead,
Love's sunshine on us would pour,
  On no one else would it be shed.

When to others the world has grown old
  And no pleasure is in their days,
Ours would be like dreams of gold
  Or sacred Elysium in reality.

Then, come to my arms, Agnes dear,
  Mind not what others say,
Life's path before us is clear
  Naught save happiness lies in the way.

TO URSULA.

O ne'er did the rolling sea
Hold a gem as fair as thee.

Ne'er was there a South-sea isle
Lovely as thy amaranthine smile.

Ne'er did there a star in boreal skies
Glisten like thy dark eyes.

Ne'er was there a mass of gold
Half so doric as thy soul.

Ne'er did the lyre of Euterpe
Sing of mortal lovely as thee.

Thou art the bard's theme
The artist's model, my fondest dream.

TO NIGHT.

Thou art the generator of gods and men,
   All we possess spring from thee.
At thy shrine in supplication we bend
   As we naturally love that which is unholy,
And what a battle we have to fight
In annulling our allegiance with thee a night.

Thy station as represented by Pausanias, a Greek
     traveller,
   Is that of a woman holding in her right hand
A white child, reposing soundly, while in the other
   A black child, likewise reposing, and
With both legs distorted. The interpretation
We believe is understood by every nation,

The white child is Sleep, the black Death.
  The woman thou, Night, nurse
Of them both. Yea, dark Night, thy breath,
  Withers fair buds that soon would burst
Into fragrant flowers. In the season thou doth con-
    trol
Christ, like a thief, will come and claim the soul.

In thy sombre presence thieves commit crime,
  Each avenue to hell is open wide,
Seductive music, sparkling wine,
  Behest onward that woeful tide,
Pressing rapaciously to that bourne
Where lost ones never cease to mourn.

TO THE MEMORY OF HENRY KIRKE WHITE.

" Fifty years hence, and who will hear of Henry ? "
  This time has already elapsed, youthful bard,
And to-day thou art as fresh in the World's memory
 As in those trying seasons when you strove so hard,
Oppressed with dreadful odds, with your lyre
To engender poesy that wouldn't evanescently expire.

Well thou didst sing, and as sublime a lay
  As he who courts the muses throughout life,
His mortal harp so worn is put away,
  And attuned to heaven's songs. No strife,
Grief, or wrong is ever harped, but thereon
By invisible fingers is played heaven's diapason.

Thy mortal harp, so pure and harmonious,
  I know it must still entrance other ears,
And in those glad hallelujahs of the just ;
  It sings not of death—a world of tears,
But of those happy celestial scenes
Whose splendor we never dream.

TO ARABELLA.

I ask thee, dear Arabella,
   Is there a fount of joy,
A fount whose crystal nectar,
   With sorrow is unalloyed.

From Pleasure's fount I quaffed,
   Which filled my soul with gladness;
Ah! how jocund I laughed,
   Till dawned the hour of sadness.

Askest not why I am sad,
   Sadness is my only heritage;
But if I thy innocence had,
   I would at once be assuaged.

Once I loved the giddy world,
   But she failed to love me,
And at my heart she hurled
   A venemous javelin—Misanthropy.

But deem not I am ill-fated,
   For O, what crowds in every zone,
Akin to myself, whose wretchedness hath created
   Within their hearts a hell of its own.

TO A FACTORY GIRL.

Come, Jennie, as the day is fine,
Why not leave your monotonous task,
On yon hill in the glad sunshine,
Where kine themselves bask;
There blooms many a lovely wild flower,
Whose fragrance would shorten these dismal hours,

Here in this close, dingy room,
Where you have toiled for many a day,
Till on your cheek there is no bloom,
Your health is fast ebbing away;
Ah! soon the time may come
When complete will be your earthly mission.

Happy are these swift revolving wheels,
The pangs of weariness they never feel,
Nor do they solicit daily bread,
Like those by your hands are fed;
Such hands of so delicate a mold
Minister to the wants of the young and old.

Your father and mother, decrepit with old age,
Against them disease doth war wage,
For their daily bread look to thee.
Your young brother and sister, from care so free,
Know little how comes their food,
But they praise you with childish gratitude.

TO MY HEART.

My heart, 'tis sad to realize,
    That thee and I must, ere long,
Sever these fond ties,
    Bound by life's fragile thong.

And when this thong parts,
    Shall we know each other more?
Thou wilt descend, poor Heart,
    To the abode of those gone before.

There, in that mysterious land,
    Wilt thou bleed and lament
Over Friendship's mutable band,
    Which is so evanescent.

Thou wilt become as earth,
   And sleep that protracted sleep
Till He who gave thee birth
   Will bid thee again beat.

Pierced by the arrows of sin,
   Polluted by all that contaminates life,
For thee there is an aim to win,
   Which wilt protect thee from strife.

Yearn not for worldly fame,
   For it will inevitably perish;
Into forgetfulness will pass those names,
   That we now devoutly cherish.

Into forgetfulness all will sink;
   The earth herself will become gray with age,
And, like mortal, tremble on the brink:
   Death is her fee-simple heritage.

TO BELINDA.

We have loved, we have parted,
   We may never meet again;
I am sad, broken-hearted,
   All hopes are rent in twain.

My heart is sort of pusillanimous,
   O'er thee 'twill forever grieve;
If another Cupid dart through it be thrust,
   'Twill be as a tongue that deceives.

Those fond dreams we indulged in,
   May they never have euthanasia,
Nor let them be scattered by the wind,
   Like Autumn leaves o'er the leaway.

Thy smiles are still as sweet,
  Bliss-inspiring as eternity in paradise ;
They may prove the acme of deceit,
  A cockatrice is in all other maids' eyes.

How I love to hear thee sing ;
  All other voices are as a wail from Erebus,
Or Lucifer's blasphemy, with weary wing,
  In descending to where dwell the unjust.

Those tresses on which much time you spent
  Trying to induce them to curl,—
To possess the like her locks of serpents
  Medusa would give, in fact, the whole infernal
    world.

Thy face, in which great beauty is,
  Is yet my idol, my all ;
To gaze on it, then on the Furies,
  No harm to the gazer could befall.

If on poor Ixion thou chanced to smile
  He would stop on his wheel
And marvel at the style
  Which from the Graces thou didst steal.

Thou promised leal friendship,
  Never to become an enemy ;
With my bruised heart may I sip
  Kind regards from the bowl with thee.

I solicit thy friendship
  And repine o'er the sad aspect ;
By the rays of affection's lamp we lit
  No deception can I detect.

Thou may extinguish the flame
  With premeditated breath,
Good-will shall be the bane
  That chills my joy to death

At the loss of a single friend I would repine,
　As friendship is the symbol of loyalty.
The same that immutable heart of thine,
　Or in mid-summer a tranquil sea.

Confide in the human heart—
　In it there is no deception,
When it has no other part
　It attests unchanging affection.

That which one day wins our admiration,
　And the next prompts us to applause,
Is Joy stepping from out her station,
　And treading underfoot gewgaws.

May this epistle give thee no offense,
　As I intend no harm;
To sing of thee is a sort of recompense
　While my muse it greatly charms.

Here allow me to insinuate—
　For ere long I must close—
Above all things choose not a mate
　To whom the muses are favorably disposed.

They might inspire him to write,
　At which the critic would cry " Asinas ad lyram ! "
If in reading a friend took delight,
　The dullness would soon tire him.

However, such is not the case,
　As I heard in recent days gone by,
That Love is ever Janus-faced,
　And possesses venom of the Hydra.

To the wilderness, like John the Baptist, I may go,
　Be doomed to subsist on locust and wild honey,
And no other pleasure will I know
　Than thinking of thee and a little pocket-money.

Bless the dreams that disturb my slumber,
　Of what thou wert in the past,
And thanks to dreams without number
　That proclaim love does always last.

TO THE SAME.

So you are happy with your new lover,
　Vowing you could never love again,—
Not when one love affair is over,
　By no means, all else is vain.

Sweet is the hive stored with honey
　Sweet is friendship when to hypocrisy unacquainted,
Sweet are relations, especially their money,
　When Mammon from us has fled.

Sweet is life, sweeter when early wed
　To our heart's first choice ;
Then Juno lays a hand on our head,
　At numerous offspring bids us rejoice.

Sweet it must be to die young,
　Then we may be sure the gods love us.
Sweet is the praise of tongues
　That at our back do not curse.

'Tis sweet when in our sky
　No ominous clouds appear,
And sweeter still is woman's eye
　When she sheds an uncollusive tear.

Her vows are unquestionably sweet,
　Seeming composed of more than words,
The heart that in her bosom beats
　Proclaims truest fidelity ever uttered.

TO IXION.

Why longer revolve on that wheel?
　'Tis but an empty task you're at,
No applause arises from the common weal,
　'Tis all bestowed on the acrobat.

The offence that you exasperate
　By Mammon's aid in these corrupt days,
You could Justice checkmate
　And win a place in the dime museum always.

Still you must revolve forever,
　The same as the world goes round,
When the vulture ceases to gnaw at Prometheus' liver,
　You and he will be unbound.

TO MORS.

Thou awful goddess, ban of all mankind,
　To thee no door is ope,
Not a single friend canst thou find,
　Though round every hearth ye grope.

To bar ye out and banish thee
　To every expedient we resort,
And when, thinking ourselves free,
　Behold! we have fallen short.

A son of the Æsculapian art
　We call unto our aid,—
'Tis vain, and with braving heart
　We stand at bay, dismayed.

When ye touch the afflicted's brow,
　O what a change is wrought;
All breathless is the dear one now,
　And our tears availeth naught.

The acme of inexorability, O Mors,
  Thou hast been since our fallen race
On that fatal day broke Jehovah's laws,
  The Tree of Life began to waste.

Thou wert, as yet, templeless abhorred
  When superstition did enshrine
Within its own fantastic orb
  Temples unto gods divine.

" The greatest of evils," thee we designate ;
  But without thy unsolicited favor
We ne'er could enter that heavenly state,
  Once by a tower we did endeavor.

Ah! thee a witch once did defy
  In calling one from out the **grave ;**
Alas! he sank back to lie,
  Till the sea its dead hath **gave.**

All hail Him who took away thy sting
  And rent asunder the shroud ;
Behold! the King of kings
  Ascended far beyond the clouds.

To Him alone is given
  Mastery over thee for a thousand years ;
This earth shall become as heaven,
  Without death, sin, or tears.

A FAREWELL ADDRESS.

Columbia ! my native land,
  Of all realms noblest and the best ;
I wert nurtured by thy benign hand,
  In thy bosom I found joy and rest.

But now the time hath come
　　That I must proclaim Adieu,
And on the set of sun
　　I'll be out on distant waters blue.

For none save thee have I a tear,
　　For none save thee will I sigh;
And as ye from sight disappear
　　I shall turn away with tearful eye.

O could I weep as I wept
　　When Hope's fount went dry;
But tears are certainly inept,
　　Save in woman's or an infant's eye.

The morn is beautiful, fair the breeze,
　　The ponderous engine is in motion;
Adown the bay by swift degrees
　　We glide toward the broad ocean.

The noble flag streams from astern,
　　It, too, sighs, Farewell! Adieu!
For thee it doth ever yearn,
　　Thy shore fast recedes from view.

Columbia! all of thee we can now behold
　　Is a dim outline against the sky,
Which unfringes the waves that roll
　　Their froth-capped forms on high.

Ah! from sight thou hast passed,
　　But in my heart thou art plain;
How speeds the ship before the gentle blast
　　That angers slightly the rolling main.

On every hand is the salt sea
　　And not a sail in sight,
The petrel on wings so free
　　Swoop the waves in delight.

O'er and round us hovers the sea-mew,
   Resting not its graceful pinions;
Soaring with vigor ever new,
   Sweet bird of Neptune's dominions!

The sun hath settled 'neath the foam
   And Twilight is at its meridian,
But how soon in Night's gloam
   This mellow-lighted season grows wan.

To myself I am left alone,
   In joyous contemplation or to sigh;
But why laugh or groan?
   The world I have passed by.

We will behold nought save sky and brine,
   The same as a fortnight through;
And, alas! 'twill not be mine,
   The land that's to gladden our view.

I care not what land it may be,
   Whether desolate or wondrously fair;
For where'er I might flee
   I would behold only Despair.

LEATHER SUSPENDERS.

Across the foot-board of my bed lie two straps,
   Sweat-stained and well worn;
To-day is Sunday, from their nap
   On the morrow they will be torn
For a whole week. Why, bless my stars!
Sleep on, old leather suspenders.

I am certain you did your duty
   Long before I were born,
My grandsire often wore thee

When his mortal day was yet at dawn ;
His career, so long and cloudy,
At length like snow melted away.

When his race was well-nigh run
     He called in an attorney and made a will,
Bequeathing the suspenders to his oldest son,
     Whose soul with misery was filled
When they were laid across his back
Till the skin was all blue and black.

This promising youth was my pa,
     Who laid them by in a chest to repose,
Till the breaking out of the civil war
     When he enlisted to vanquish the foe
That many a gallant Yankee did shoot,
He put them on with his Sunday suit.

In the wild, tumultuous din of battle,
     Where dying men shrieked, musketry cracked
          treble,
Sabres clashed, bayonets gleamed, artillery rattled ;
     With the suspenders he slew the rebels ;
They withered 'neath the blows like grass,
Or like Philistines that Samson slew with the jaw-
          bone of an ass.

When the rebel flag at Appomatox was forever
          furled,
     They were presented to General Grant,
Who wore them on his tour around the world ;
     When the Goddess of Liberty began to pant
Because the great General's wealth was gone,
She righted his circumstances by placing them in
          pawn,

Be it known that I the great *I am*,
    Around whom revolve few inferior satellites,
Did the pawnbroker's purse with money cram,
    And took the suspenders home in delight.
I intend to hang them from a peg on my library wall,
Where they will remain till after I am from existence
      called.

A LOVER'S LAMENT AT HIS SWEET-
HEART'S GRAVE.

Can it be that she, the joy of this brief day,
    Reposes 'neath this grassy mound,
Whereon long grasses to the winds sway,
    That rush through the wood with mournful sound?

Only as yesterday, it seems to me,
    Though it is a score and half years ago,
On an inclement November day, that we
    Laid her at rest 'mid the falling snow.

Those large white flakes from dark clouds fell,
    Covering the sea and earth, were not more pure
Than that soul, which so brief a spell
    In its own happy castle dwelt secure.

She died in her joyant prime
    When life in each vicissitude teems with joy,
When our mortal sun the brightest shines,
    Our fondest hopes Death so oft destroys.

She died when all without was aged,
    The earth was clad in a wintry mantle,
The warm sky was decayed from o'erhead,
    And harsh winds from the North swelled,

She died when so beautiful, alas !
   All lovely flowers doth early perish,
While noxious ones stem cold blasts,
   And severe frosts they seem to cherish.

She died when Death would have claimed
   Many others (if taking cognizance of years),
But the decrepit form he disdains,
   To behold stretched stark upon his bier.

The tall pine in the yard,—'neath its boughs
   She oft sought shelter from the summer sun—
Sighed and moaned as if it could not allow
   Its intense grief another moment to run.

Her canary with ruffled feathers sat in its cage,
   And at intervals twittered a dirge ;
By these doleful notes the sufferer was assuaged,
   And from all pain seemed purged.

When her life was ebbing like some river,
   Gently pouring o'er its broad sandy bed,
Methought I heard voices from the mystical Forever
   Proclaiming that joy awaits the righteous dead.

When her life was ebbing gently,
   O, the sad hearts that round her couch assembled !
Their last message of love to pay ;
   Strong eyes wept and strong voices trembled.

Her small hand, of perfection's mold,
   By which the famishing were oft appeased,
I clasped in mine.   O, it was so cold !
   All wasted by deleterious disease.

Could this be the hand that I
  So often clasped in gladsome days of yore ;
A rill of merriment ran from those eyes,
  O'er which now pale heavy lids were lower'd.

Those cheeks in which beauty bloomed,
  From them disease had chased it away ;
When Death calls us to the tomb,
  No color in the face doth stay.

Her brow, curtained with sunny curls,
  Was unchanged, save a whiter hue ;
Not a furrow was thereon. The world
  To her was yet new.

Those eyes, mild as a gazelle's,
  Had lost their Promethean fire,
And stared vacantly at intervals :
  They bespoke she was about to expire.

From those pale lips came
  No words of farewell,
But a smile expressed the same,
  That long on her countenance did dwell.

Her breath grew short and labored :
  A faint gasp—a sweet smile,—
A silence—nothing more was heard,
  Her spirit was with God ere this while.

O could it be she had yielded up the ghost,
  Without a word, a murmur, or a groan ?
Like some tranquil sea impinging its coast,
  Her spirit passed into the great unknown.

O God ! Could it be that she, the joy,
  The pride of my youthful years,
By Death was so soon destroyed,
    Leaving me to grope alone through the vale of
      tears ?

ISLANDS OF THE BLEST.

I glean from the bards of old
   There are islands in the **West,**
The abode of happy souls,
   Islands of the Blest.

Islands of the Blest,
   On thee the sun ever shines
No storm clouds gather in the **West**
   To chill the amaranth or eglantine.

Mong amaranthine bowers dwell
   Birds of song, sweeter thrice
Than the linnet or philomel,
   Of plumage like the bird of **paradise.**

Death, disease, sorrow and care
   Are all sunken in the sea,
Their roomy bed they share
   With woe throughout eternity.

With thee there is no night,
   Nor do cold winds ever moan,
Crystal streams flow on in delight,
   Like the river before the Omnipotent's throne.

Where are those pestilences, famines and wars
   That so often devast our earth?
They, like the despot's laws,
   With thee never had a birth.

Hearts that have become sear
   With miseries of old age forsooth,
Eyes that are dim with the tear,
   Partake of the boon—perpetual youth.

From Lethe's oblivious stream
  They quaff, and O, what a change !
The past vanishes like a dream
  When Morpheus inspires us with nothing strange.

Every woe of earth is past,
  The season of strife is o'er,
Joy, peace and happiness doth amass
  Each tenant of this tranquil shore.

O, Islands of the Blest,
  Thou art heaven indeed !
A haven for the weary to rest
  Where no broken heart e'er bleeds.

NOTHING NEW UNDER THE SUN.

There's nothing new under the sun :
  The winds blow the same as on creation's morn,
Over the same channels streams run,
  At eve the sun goes to his bourne,
And in the morn when he reappears,
His rays doth all nature cheer.

The stars that beautify the night
  On the break of day grow dim,
The green fields become white
  When snows fall, and winter winds
In their fury rage just the same
Ere man into existence came.

The ocean waves roll and tides ebb
  With their ancient punctiliousness,
The volcano with its blazing head
  Doth the same energy manifest ;
Rugged hills retain their ancient forms
Notwithstanding the many devastating storms.

Man builds his abode of granite, brick, and forest-trees.
   Many a city, town, hamlet is scattered o'er the plains,
But Time wastes each by slow degrees.
Green grows the grass on the spot
Where stood the king's palace and peasant's cot.

There's nothing new under the sun.
   No, nothing!   Life is just the same thing
Since the Fates their first thread spun ;
   Atropos' shears still sever the vital string,
Which she will continue to clip incessantly
Until the heavens and earth pass away.

THE FOUNTAIN OF YOUTH.

O, who hath not heard the story forsooth
Of Ponce de Leon seeking the Fountain of Youth
'Mid Florida's many a stagnant pool?
But he found it not,—the old fool.

He found it not where Spanish moss hangs
O'er water's brow like a lady's bangs,
Not in the mud where alligators creep,
Where swamp fever its vigil keeps.

He found it not 'mid blooming flowers
That blossom in wintry bowers,
But found it when short was his breath,
And gazed upon it through the portal of death.

WHEN I THAT COLD BREATHLESS SLEEP TAKE.

When I that cold breathless sleep take,
May Asclepios from it me ne'er awake.
Who is he, after having life's labyrinth run.
Would exchange the pleasure of Elysium
For these few days of pain and sorrow
Which death may end on the morrow?

There's rest in the grave. O grave,
O'er thee the tree Forgetfulness doth wave,
And Lethean dews nourish the grass
That grows thereon.   The frosts, alas !
Chill to death the flowers planted by loving hands,
Which cherish all that death leaves in this land.

Friend and foe fade alike from our view,
And enter upon a mysterious existence new ;
What that may be ask not mortal,
For no pilgrim has ever returned by Death's portal.
The most profound philosopher has clearly shown,
" All we know is, nothing can be known."

As nothing can be known for certainty,
Why should we imagine great evils await us in
     eternity?
Dust we are and to dust we return.
Forgetfulness doth remembrance of us burn,
Till by the world we are wholly forgot,
Whether glorious or inglorious was our lot.

MOUNT OBLIVION.

Beyond the horizon of our mortal sky,
In spectral gloom, a lofty mountain lies,
O'er whose crest hover darkest clouds of night
That no glad sunbeams ever light.

Upon its scorched, barren sides.
Not a tree or blade of grass thrives ;
No crystal torrents adown precipices leap,
Resounding rhythmically through gorges deep.

Far beneath it, where gnomes dream,
Flows tumultuously Lethe's stream,—
The only true antidote for deeds of woe,
That oft makes the Past an inferno.

From each of the winds of heaven four,
Through gloom that to the base lowers,
Come multitudes. Poor, careworn souls,
Seeking rest at Life's oblivious goal.

Into the earth's cold bosom sinks this mighty host,
Weeping and wailing, then to give up the ghost.
However few there be of ambition yet sublime
That strive manfully the summit to climb.

In the ebon shades horrid, dismal,
Lose their way on the sides abysmal,
Round and round they wander, at length to sink
O'er one of the many precipices' brink.

" O Son of Man ! " a sage cries,
" Our race is run, for here we die ;
This last hour in Him put thy trust,
'Tis well that we return to dust."

" Not yet, O Father, Hope proclaims a different story ;
On the crest I'll unfurl my faded standard of glory,
That long waved o'er land and sea,
To which millions bent a supplicant knee."

Thus replied one of kingly mien,
Who once a mundane god had been ;
Upward went he and two comrades with might,
And, ere long, paused upon a rugged height.

Thus rang first speaker's voice, proud and strong :—
" O, immortal gods, my glorious reign was long ;
By fire, famine and the sword nations I conquered.
The orphan's cry and widow's wail on every hand
          was heard.

" On scores of gory battlefields
The foe was stretched stark upon his shield ;
At midnight the glare of consuming cities and towns
Glowed as a diadem in Ambition's crown.

"Pale, wan Famine followed pillage and flame,
Young ravens for food called on God's name;
From fields of carnage, from manifold woes,
From vacant thrones a Tamerlanean pyramid arose.

"On the pyramid's crest I burned incense to my glory
            high,
Inscribing my name in letters of fire on Fame's sky.
Alas! all suddenly changed to wormwood or aloe,
And took wings like Riches that upward go."

He paused, fell prostrate; his spirit had fled,
A doleful gale his requiem chanted;
The multitude below derided and cursed his name.
An unscrupulous aspirant was he who sought worldly
            fame.

The second speaker, of demeanor somewhat meek,
In mild, clear accent thus did speak :—
"To my memory naught will remain, I know,
For on tablets of air I wrote, with pen of snow.

"The glory of our monarch, theme of our age,
I inscribed with eloquence on Clio's sacred page;
And now, since Wrong to Right must yield,
Oblivion sets upon the whole her seal."

On taking a step up the rugged steep,
He sank down to repose, as we all must sleep,
Beside his fallen comrade the third speaker stood
Calmly as rustles the breeze of eve through the wood.

Upon him gazed the multitude; with loud acclaim
They applauded. On every lip was his name;
The respect shown him seem to state
That he was a mighty potentate.

Began he "My days hath been all of resplendent
        sheen,
As from Life's great field I gleaned ;
After the reaper I bound the golden sheaves,
And odorous was the zephyr as e'er breathes.

" At eve, when o'er was my pleasant lot,
I retired to my thatched cot,
And there, round my knee,
Children gathered with smiles of glee.

" With a lovely harp of mine
Many a garland I did entwine
Round the column of Memory,
Which from Envy's spots art free.

" To the sad in heart I sung a lay
Of good times in bygone days
Before the heavy hand of care
Stamps the brow pure and fair.

" To him encumbered with strife
I sang of peace of life,
Of a land of bliss,
Where there are no tears, as in this."

With a smile he passed away,
His bones beside his comrades lay ;
The multitude below yet mourn,
He was one of the few that doth earth adorn.

A PESSIMIST'S ARGUMENT.

How solemn and deep this inmost thought
That's enthralled within my breast ;
'Tts as some immutable cataract's roar
That adaws the tranquil hour of Night ;
Or, like the noonday sun that becomes wan

In skies momentarily ago benign;
Or as fair young leaves that wither,
When Spring endows the Universe with new life.

But why further contemplate? The whole category
Of human affairs are contradictory as when ominous
    thunder
Resonant, proclaims to the parched earth
A copious fall of rain ; but a fierce sunbeam
Shoots forth, and behests the clouds to disperse.
A diaphanous mist, which the eye doth easily
    penetrate,
May obfuscate the high, towering mount's crest,
When we are wont to gaze upon some sublime object
Attesting the grandeur of the Invisible's design.
Man's most consummate plans are swallowed up
By the quicksands of his own natal obduracy ;
The Golden Rule becomes as a taskmaster's lash
In the hands of an indefatigable fiend incarnate
Soon as Obligation retires to his unobligatory couch ;
Charity, the mitigator of manifold ills,
Augments, to a supercilious stranger,
The moment a philanthropic deed remains unveiled,
To a multitude of pompostus plaudits.
The desideratum—Parental affection, Brotherly love,
Was chilled to death by the first inclement blast
That wafted heavenward the Tree of Life's sear
    leaves,
After fallen Man had fled beneath the ban of death.

DR. MARY WALKER'S ORATION OVER THE REMAINS OF MISS BUSTLE.

Dear Sisters: This very morn, as the sun gilded the
    horizon,
Threads of silver and chains of golden light melted
    into one.

Night in her sable chariot drove rapidly toward the
        West;
Meadow, glen, hill and mount in a bright mantle was
        dressed;
A fleet of fleecy clouds floated low.   Nature with joy
        was ready to overflow;
But, alas! 'mid such splendor there's profound sorrow.

We are assembled for saddest lamentation,
To mourn a cause that recks the throne of nations,
The ghost of Cæsar has not returned to cross the
        Rubicon
Nor has the South engendered another insurrection.
O Sisters! this bundle of wire its own sad story will
        tell—
The mortal remains of angelic Miss Bustle.

A single enemy she had not, the whole feminine monde
        her death will deplore,
From she who sways Albion's sceptre down to the
        servant-girl scrubbing the cellar-door.
Aye! by old maids she was devoutly cherished,
Who have seen their twenty-first set of false teeth
        perish;
Children upon her their juvenile affections shed,
Who still repose in the trundle bed.

O Sisters!   Our great benefactress is gone!
Her remains are soon to be taken by the monarch
        Fashion,
And interred in a mouldy chest in the back-room,
Where not a sunbeam smiles on the gloom ;   ·
And as on her grave we cannot strew a flower,
O let our tears flow in this sad, dark hour.

The blushing school-ma'am was her truest friend,
And here weeps saddest o'er her end ;
The young dashing grass-widow was her maid of honor
While the old portly lady, her humiliating donner,

'Twas a ridiculous sight to behold a frump
By the aid of Mrs. Bustle supporting a camel's hump.
Ah, Sisters, she was a friend in whom we could confide,
Being, by the will of Providence, Constancy's bride.

Sisters, not to find fault with one of you this oration
    I deliver,
There is not a fault-finding arrow in my whole quiver,
But merely to enumerate and extol the deceased's
    virtues.
Just as she had passed Fashion's labyrinth through,
And sought in vain for quietude on society's tumul-
    tuous shore,
Fashion smote her, and she breathed no more.

'Tis natural our tears should flow,
The last ray of comfort has received a fatal blow.
To Fashion's edict we must yield us as slaves,
And pursue the monarch like ocean waves follows
    wave,
Till at last we become useless like this bundle of wire,
And, like angelic Miss Bustle, we expire.

A NOVEMBER EVE.

The moon in the hazy sky
    Looks down on the sere earth,
And winds with boreal voices sigh,
    As if applauding harsh Winter's birth.

A lurid cloud passes o'er her face ;
    The land is clad in Night.
Now from the North, with rapid pace,
    Comes many a moonbeam bright ;
The cloud floats South and East,
And no other cloud comes to break her face.

Yellow is the forest and fields of corn,—
    The whole land seems clad in gold.
The silvery moonbeams seem to scorn
    That they are not of so valuable a mold.
The breeze that passes on to a sunny clime
Is both gold and silver lined.

A FOE.

Like Ponce de Leon seeking the Fountain of Youth,
    In the wild drear morass of Florida,
Through many a land I wander in sooth,
    Striving to chase melancholy away.

Where'er I go the tormentor is there
    In each hour of both Day and Night,
He and his inseparable comrade—Despair,
    In tormenting me ever take delight.

To the festival and banquet I go,
    Where assemble the young and gay,
Through Retrospection comes this foe
    To extinguish Pleasure's last ray.

The beaker I fill to the brim,
    And drain its last exhilarating dregs,
When chairs and tables round me spin,
    This for my attention begs.

Far in the primeval forest I stroll
    Where seldom tread human feet,
When thinking myself secure behold!
    This foe and I do meet.

MY HOME.

The silvery moon is gleaming
    O'er distant hill-tops high,
And of home I am dreaming,
    That I bade good-bye.

My home, so far away,
  Is by the deep blue sea,
Where sunbeams mingle with spray,
  And where breakers roar with glee.

Round my home are flowery hills
  On which happy children play.
In the shady wood by sparkling rills
  Lambs rest at sultry noonday.

O'er my home smile bluest skies,
  And birds sing their sweetest songs
From out of some tree-top high
  In the meadow or the hedge along.

At my home loved ones dwell,
  There Affection's flambeau brightly burns;
By loving hands 'twill be guarded well
  Till a lone wanderer returns.

THANKSGIVING.

Some two hundred and odd score years have fled
  Since upon New England's barren coast forlorn,
These few starving devout Pilgrims were fed
  From the Indians' meagre hoard of corn.

The Red man, whom we bitterly detest,
  And hunt down like some beast of prey
On this event our nation blessed,
  Giving us glorious Thanksgiving Day.

This is the day to offer up thanks
  To Him who rules on high, ·
For our wealth in the bank,
  For roast turkey and mince-pie.

With our friends we go out to dine
  And sup till we can hold no more.
Perchance in a beaker of wine
  We drink his health o'er and o'er.

Then we feel kingly in our lowly station,
  And soar aloft on wings hilarious;
In our wild state of intoxication
  We disdain to tread the dust.

When these mirthful hours have melted into night,
  We take our best girl to the ball;
To enchanting music 'neath brilliant lights
  Waltz, schottische, and obey the prompter's call

But, O, when next day comes about,
  We deem life hardly worth the living;
We have headache, an attack of gout,
  Brought on by glorious Thanksgiving.

THE PARTING.

'Twas on a clear, cold February eve
  That a young pair came together,
To take a farewell leave,
  To meet again, O never!

There were no cheery words spoken,
  As in blithesome days for aye gone;
The silence at intervals was broken
  By words sharp as an orange thorn.

Eyes that looked undying love
  Were wroth with anger filled,
Akin to those unsleeping Ones above
  When His forbearance is chilled.

The hand so fondly proffered
  Was cold, heavy like stone,
Despite when it was offered
  Affection o'er it brightly shone.

Lips that murmured of perpetual bliss,
  Stable as the duration of Eternity,
Had nought to say but this :—
  "Alas! 'twas not to be!"

What wrought this change dire?
  Was it that Love had grown old,
Wanting the Promethean fire
  That enraptures the youthful soul?

O no! 'Twas a galling tongue
  Possessed by a nefarious Até;
Slander by the hypocrite was flung,
  And it fell with fatal weight.

It fell burning to the ground,
  As falls God's just wrath,
In two hearts inflicting a wound,
  In Life's course two separate paths.

She trod the path, forsooth,
  That a lovelorn maid usually takes—
Being wooed and won by another youth—
  And her heart no longer breaks.

Ah, but he doth pursue a way
  Long and broad as the Universe,
Like the Hebrew wanderer of olden days
  To plod onward 'neath a curse.

Yet, he doth not wear the willow,
  Nor repine along the way,
His grief is sunken 'neath the billow,
  Far from the sun's faintest ray.

But as he presses on and on,
  Life hath a sombre hue,
Like when the sun is gone,
  When tranquil eve sheds her dew.

6

In many a clime he may sojourn,
    Mingle with the light-hearted and gay ;
Still in his bosom there'll burn,
    A flame of dissension for aye.

O when youth's fount is filled,
    Flowing o'er with peace and joy,
What hopes upon sand we build,
    That a drop of rain will oft destroy

Proclaim not that love is perpetual,
    That it ever found lodgment in the breast,
'Mong mortals 'twas ne'er designed to dwell,
    'Tis heaven's most distinguished guest.

AN OBJECT OF DREAD.

Talk no more about pleasure in the crowded city,
Where pomp and pride are at the meridian,
Where soft eyes so full of love and pity
Enchant each passer-by, and in those dens
What crowds of erring mortals full of lust,
Open a way for the innocent to Erebus.

Talk no more about the parlor with its furniture,
In the centre where sits your sweetheart's mamma,
Who weighs each word spoken.   Each gesture
She approves or disapproves, and her daughter,
Of course, cannot get a word in edgewise,
While that loquacious tongue of hers to perfection
    flies.

Talk no more about the vigilant bull-dog
That guards our possessions from the midnight thief,
Nor of the unmerciful fathers that flog

Us youth, and crown our brow with a wreath
Of harsh words; all these are naught
When in contact with your sweetheart's wrathy Pa,
    you're brought.

WORLDLY AMBITION.

The traveller who ascends earth's loftiest mount
Is impeded by perpetual snow. The atmosphere
    stings
As if winter from Arctic regions hath taken wings.
On gazing below he beholds green forests, and founts
Sending forth crystal streams—a landscape
To which eternal Summer is a mate.

Perchance a week or month he hath spent
Mid great peril, in gaining this lofty altitude,
Simply to say that he alone hath stood
Where no mortal ever trod before. Yet, not content,
He ascends higher to where his comrades can
Behold him and exclaim—" Of men he's the man!"

Of men he's the man, but what of that?
The simple mound of earth outlasts
His Fame, Fortune, and his all. Green grows the
    grass
Where mighty Babylon once stood, and at
Some period, maybe not very remote,
Our cities will all crumble to naught.

In ruins will smoulder our treasures,
Our virtues and vices. All that we love or hate
To desolation and oblivion will be mates.
Should some fragments remain, in the measure
Of antiquity, by nations to come, they will be cast
Like those of the Mound Builders—a race from us
    passed.

VAINGLORIOUS SALMONEUS.

'Tis recorded of Salmoneus that he was unsatisfied
With an earthly crown, but yearned for divine honors.
That people might deem him a god he built a far
Spanning bridge over the city whereon he did drive
With his chariot, by this noise imitating Jupiter's
    thunder,
That still makes us quake with fearful wonder.

At the same time he cast flaming torches among
The multitude below, imitating lightning—many
    were killed,
At such imposition Jupiter with wrath was filled,
And he cast this vainglorious wretch to where no
    tongue
Can describe the woes of hell. So much
For striving to grasp that which he couldn't touch.

FRIENDLY ADVICE TO A POET.

You unfortunate mortal twanging the Lyre,
Striving to pour forth your inspiration,
I beseech you at once to shun
Such a calling, for you will surely tire
The patience of both critic and friend,
Who will at you missiles of Derision send.

Poet, what is the reward
For your laborious compiled volumes ?
'Tis but the presence of the Furies who fume
Their wrath on you—or to be gnawed
By extreme poverty. While your mortal sun is yet
    high,
Up in that garret you will die.

Your works, what becomes of them ?
Unread, they are laid by on a dusty shelf
Or cast in the waste basket. Such pelf
Alone is yours. Those works that stem
The critics' opinion, and at every fireside are sung,
Will inevitably be lost 'mong the confusion of tongues

THE PHILOSOPHER'S STONE.

In a vision before me rises a hill,
A proclivious hill, considerably more round
Than oval, shaped like an egg, but still
It is, most too round ; and three sides bound
Agitated waves of a wide extending sea
That for ages hath not known a moment's tranquillity.

On its rugged sides are trees,
Forest trees, gigantic and old ; those
That are most ancient seem pleased
At their enormous growth. Huge vines, foes
To the young forest monarchs,
Girdle many times their gnarly trunks.

This primeval forest with evergreens is dappled
And at intervals are small clearings—the
Work of man. Here the peach, plum and apple
Shed their choice fruit. It is a pleasant sight to see
These fruits when matured, their deliciousness
Seems by celestial fragrance blest.

There the wild grape grows in profusion
Suspending its tempting fruit from some big branch ;
An attempt to pluck a cluster would seem intrusion
On the grandeur of the scene. And, as if by chance,
Several small fields of yellow grain
Their beauteous aspect on this landscape rain

Wherever a forest monarch hath cast off a branch,
Against it brilliant flowers support their slender forms,
And as if by the command of Providence
They wither not, nor do furious storms
Prostrate or snap their stems asunder.   Such are
Their beauties, painted by the hand of the Creator.

On the crest of this hill there's a tower,
Nearly a complete ruin.   On approaching it
I discover a sage.   It seems that my hours
Would scarcely equal his years.   And yet,
This cannot be.   I know very well
He is the oldest man I ever beheld.

He is so bowed, I cannot ascertain
Whether it is the result of years or a deformity ;
Each step, short and slow, produces him pain.
On reaching the bottom of the crumbling stairs he
Calls in a piping voice to know
If to the top of the tower I wish to go.

Being somewhat startled at his request,
I reply, " Father, I am in search of Truth,
And if within thy tower, such age doth manifest ;
Thou hast it concealed. I will enter forsooth—"
He straightened up and smiled ironically.
Up the stairs he led the way.

The stairs were winding, up and up we went,
It seemed as if the top would ne'er be gained,
'Twas like ascending to the top of Bunker Hill mon-
        ument
E'er whose top is reached fatigue explains
Why laborious is an upward flight,—
Souls that have not toiled and striven ne'er attain a
        lofty height.

At length we reached the top and entered an apart-
    ment,
Scattered over the stone floor and in large heaps
Were various pieces of old iron, bars of copper; some
    were bent
In odd shape.   This individual kept a stone as keeps
The miser his gold—this he called the Philosopher's
    Stone,
Which many wonderful properties did own.

He touched the stone to a large rusty anchor
Which instantly transformed it to gold—
Precious gold for which we all hanker,
And to acquire it we oft destroy our soul.
This golden anchor in less time than I can repeat
He picked up and cast it at my feet.

A VISION.

The day has not yet expired, it seems,
When young men shall see visions
And old men dream dreams.
In the rays of a visionary sun
I see in the distance a beautiful isle
On which a calm ocean smiles.

On the lone shore there's a wharf
At which a single ship lies,
And from the masts aloft
A strange pennon to the breeze flies;
Snugly furled are the sails
Like when descends a gale.

Not a soul treads the deck,
No sound proceeds from the cabin
All within is silent as a wreck
That at the bottom of the sea has been
Since the first dauntless mariner
Ventured out on seas afar.

A small village on a mountain plain
Is the only evidence of habitation,
Save few patches of yellow grain
That await the reapers, task to be down.
In the background are also few cabins rude,
That render more picturesque the solitude.

In one of these cabins dwelt a youth
Till few years ago, and hence
'is time was spent in a way uncouth,
Which ere long did recompense
Him with those chimeric rewards
Meted out to the sluggard.

Not that he was at all evil,
But much time on the seashore passed;
And when storms did swell
He exulted in their roar,
By the sea and in the wood
Indulged in his poetic mood.

He poured forth many a lay
Of such as the prosaic never think;
To the interior he took his way
To where mounts rise and torrents dash o'er their
          brink.
And here, 'mong the lone dreary heights,
He lives the life of an anchorite.

Twas so ordained by Fate
That he should leave all behind,
Distrust and misanthropic hate
Flit and hover round his mind;
Love in fetters bound
Stalks with ghastly stride his cavern around.

One by one he saw his friends depart
As they leave when friendship is hoar,
Or when hypocrisy corrodes the heart

Blighting it to the core.
Amid the wreck and waste,
Confidence stares with a Janus face.

THE CORNER LOT.

At the far West, in the Land of Gold,
Where Owen's Lake's deleterious waters roll ;
Hard by where the rugged Inyos are
Lies the isolated village of Keeler.

East and West, far as the eye can trace,
Barren or wooded mounts fill the space ;
The grandest of all these be,
The sublimely upheaved Mount Whitney.

Alone in frigid sublimity it stands,
With an imperial beck to man ;
It invites him to thither wing
To vouch it hath no offspring.

And thou, Keeler, till shortly ago,
The same to the traveller thou could'st show ;
As rainless as is the sky o'erhead,
Within thee Nature seemed as dead.

The scion of a most hardy stock,
One of the half score to a flock,
Brought his fair young wife unto this place,
But failed to perpetuate his race.

Many became aged and at length died,
Their hoard the administrator did divide,
According to the unique will's decrees,
Benefiting friends, the Piute and heathen Chinese.

On the town and on every hand,
There seem to rest a dreadful ban ;

In the nursery no infant's smiles bloomed,
Infantine smiles alone would break the gloom.

The villager still passed away
Without a child to bemoan the fatal day;
Ere long the burial place would win them all,
Leaving Emptiness to tenant their hall.

One morn appeared this proclamation
Pasted on trees, in the railway station,
On empty dry goods boxes, on kegs of beer,
And on fences from far and near:—

" To the first white child that is begot,
I, John Barnes, do hereby agree to donate a corner lot,
The parents can choose at option
From Lake View Block to Salt-grass Lawn."

Dames assembled and discussed loquaciously,
Men, too, gathered and in their usual way
Of surmounting difficulties egregious, vast,
They indulged in many a social glass.

Father Time dealt out a year
But no claimant for the lot did appear;
Another fleeting year went by
And with it Hope began to die.

A score of years fleeted past
Still the claimant came not. Overcast
Became the effulgent sky of Hope,
In the world of the unborn the claimant was yet to
     grope.

A score and half years were meted out to Saturn,
The many prayers but nought did refute;
The wheel of Fortune would only turn
In favor of the " hogachi " soliciting Piute.

"O fellow citizens," cried Father Barnes in despair,
To all our invocations fickle Fortune is mute,
Not one of us has yet or ever will claim an heir,
Let the Corner Lot be given to the next infant Piute.

"Hold your hasty tongue yet a little while,"
Cried Madame Rumor; "there's no danger
But that Fortune will yet on us smile,
On the way to town there's a little stranger.

"Where he is to stop 'tis not for me to say,
Perhaps, Father Barnes, as everybody loves you best,
Because you feed each moneyless soul that comes this
    way,
He may be, which I hope, your guest."

"Verily I could believe this true,"
Replied Mr. Barnes, in tones sore,
"But it is apparent to both me and you
That 'mong us the Lord's favors are o'er."

"Ah, I see!" exclaimed Ernest Hall from his post
Beside his mysterious dot-talking instrument,
"Mr. and Mrs. Fiehman are to be the hosts,"
(Here he let a tear fall), "Let us be content."

And so it came about
That on no distant day,
The little stranger on his route,
Straight to "Honest John's" took his way.

What rejoicing there was in town
On this mild April morn!
Flags floated aloft, anvils did sound,
An ovation to the Claimant new-born.

Sweet to the juvenile sight is that of a menagerie
Dear to the feminine heart is perfumery, paint, pow-
    der, parasol and fans;
But far sweeter and dearer than any of these
Was the little stranger at Fiehman's.

With hearts of love somewhat, envy-filled
Came ladies who took the infant from the crib;
With caresses he was almost killed,
'Twas miraculous that through the ordeal he lived.

Then came man with grizzled phiz,
Who long had lived 'mong the mounts;
How awkward was that tongue of his
In exhausting affection's fount.

"By George!" exclaimed a stalwart miner
"'Tis the best pay streak
I have seen since the stars
Shone on me at Bodie bleak."

THE BOWL.

That which we call affection
The next day becomes cold;
Friends I claim none
Save thee, voluptuous Bowl.

O Bowl, in thee no treachery is found,
A single quaff of thy nectar
Heals the deep maculate wound
And obliterates every scar.

Thou art the only nepenthus,
Exalting man above his dismal sphere;
The king, peasant, just and unjust
All mankind thou doth cheer.

When crossed in treacherous love,
When encumbered with care,
Like an empyrean ray from above
Thou makest our pathway fair.

The buffoon in vain we employ
To make our sad moments light,
When in our melancholy alloy
The sun shineth bright.

Old feuds of long standing
Ye scatter with a smile like chaff,
When strife for slaughter art banding
At thy bidding drops his sword and laughs.

By some thou art denounced as deleterious,
An object to loath and abhor;
But thy votaries ne'er become as rust
In obeying thy exhilarating laws.

The sluggard passes his days in slumber,
The miser in the acquisition of gold,
But thy subjects their mellow days number
As the hours of mirth o'er them roll.

FRAGMENT.

The sweetest music soon dies away,
The noblest deeds are soon forgotten;
The path of true friendship is soon o'errun
With briers and noxious weeds that decay
Not when icy winds blow or frosts fall
Which doth the flowers to their bourn call.

The stars, the bright, twinkling stars,
Are oft hidden by cold storm-clouds
That o'ercast the sky in a seamless shroud
That send down missiles of ice, and, far
As the eye can penetrate, it beholds gloom,
Winds wail as if Æolus to mourn was forever doomed.

DIGNITY OF LABOR.

In the humblest walks of life there's grandeur.
Who doth not admire the sturdy husbandman
As he, with brawny arm and callous hand
Swings his scythe through the grass. The odor
Of the new-mown hay perfumes the air around him,
And sweet song birds warble from the limbs.

The laborer with sleeves rolled to his elbow
Wielding the pick or shovel doth fret
Apart the solid earth.   His brow is all a-sweat.
Every stroke he makes is an honest blow.
Slowly, but surely, he excavates an aperture
Through which will rush the car.

OUT A COURTING.

Too soon thou came, melancholy morn,
    To call me from my cozy couch,
And from out a dream that did adorn
    My brief slumber, and verily, I vouch,
It was one of the most grand
That ever escapes from fantastic Dreamland.

Where was I while others napped?
    Not poring o'er a volume of half-forgotten lore,
Nor burning my midnight lamp, enwrapped
    In jolly contemplation, nor
Sitting up with drowsy eyes
To watch the moon set and the sun rise.

Not scheming how to mold a friend
    From him who has long been a foe,
Not striving my waywardness to mend,
    Which surely needs mending, I know,
As does the sock on the foot of Time
Which has not been darned since Adam's prime,

Not fretting and worrying how on earth
   To pick a quarrel with a troublesome friend,
Not planning how to affront a neighbor whose worth,
   At borrowing, seems like eternity without an end :
He comes with dire complaints of Poverty's wrongs,
Borrows the flat-irons, skillet and tongs.

Not in a gloomy cell in jail,
   Where the long-incarcerated felon awaits his doom,
How Horror rends the midnight air with wails
   That echo through the long corridors of gloom,
And the heavy iron door on its rusty hinges
Opes by ghostly hands the wall it impinges.

Not at the banquet, mingling with the gay,
   Where Pleasure launches its bark, Hilarity,
Before Exhilaration's breeze it sails away,
   At length to be obscured by the circumbent sea.
From mortal view it has forever passed,—
Those on board an ocean of mirth amassed.

Not weighing my soul in Life's great scale,
   Whose weights have always proven categorical,
Not mourning o'er the manifold pains and ails
   That in this carnate structure of ours dwell ;
Its walls they mar and exterior deface,
And ere long the whole body goes to waste.

Why should the truth be longer withheld,
   And now I will reveal the truth.
I was where my thoughts dwell—
   Where they have dwelt since early youth,
And throughout this blissful time
Life has been of all sunshine.

Should I speak plainer still?
   I was with my sweetheart,
Seated on the doorstep of her pa's mill.
   The broad, deep waters with a start
Dashed o'er the high stone dam,
And round a bend they grew calm,

The rugged bluffs o'erlooking the river
Listed not with eager ears to what was said,
The moonbeams that on the pond did quiver
Recked not why we from the house fled.
On empty air how soon died away,
Those harsh words her father did say.

DARWINISM.

When Boreas breathes with hoar breath
On lands wrapped in universal death,
Where harsh old Winter hath his palace
In the midst of an icy waste,
This was in a long past age—the Miocene—
A delightful realm of living green.

Warm was the ocean that rolled,
Laving lands around the Pole,
With skies above all warm and bright,
Smiling ever on this realm of delight.
The fig tree showered its fruit upon the ground,
Delicious fruit everywhere did abound.

O, Miocene Age! too fair to be seen
Outside the boundary of Elysian dreams,
Why didst thou ever take wing,
Giving up thy throne to a king
Whose only pleasure is, we know,
In heaping high both ice and snow?

Gigantic was the fauna and verdant the flora,
More luxuriant than that in Eden's story.
It was, in whole, an age better far
Than that in which we now are ;.
But, despite its being so wondrously grand,
It wanted God's noblest creature—Man,

But, as years upon years went by,
Harsh winds began to sigh.
When blew the cold, benumbing gale
All life in the verdant foliage failed.
In forlorn grandeur a naked forest stood
In many respects resembling our disenrobed autumn
    wood.

Still, years upon years crept past;
The cold, benumbing gale became a boreal blast;
The dead naked forest no more was seen,
In its stead flourished the evergreen;
Dead, too, was the fauna, save the grittiest,
'Twas the survival of the fittest.

Up in an evergreen, awaiting their fate,
Were two shivering, half-starved apes—
(That no confusion may exist herein
We will call them Mr. and Mrs. Charles Darwin.
The ghost of this great evolutionist will be pleased
    indeed,
On beholding our first ancestors treed.)

For food they searched the tree-top through,
But not even a cone in it grew,
They beheld a mammoth past them rush
Bearing in uplifted trunk a machairodus
Which it dashed to death upon the ground
For trying with its terrible teeth the mammoth to
    wound.

Then came a woolly rhinoceros
Hotly pursued by two machairodus.
The chase lasted but a short way,
As the tigers overtook and killed their prey.
A hippotamus wallowed through the snow,
A musk sheep sought safety in the thicket below.

An Irish stag, a long-fronted ox,
Bounded off among the rocks.
On the tree-top still clung the shivering apes,
Planning the best course to take.
Said Mr. Darwin, " Since dead are all the elves,
Suppose we cut off our tails and hang ourselves?"

" Agreed," replied the madam ; "as all our kindred
    have died.
We might as well end our misery by suicide.
'Tis all the same, for our race is almost run."
Thus we have the first case of premeditated self-
    destruction,
Since then, from some lunatic reason, in every land
Man has sought death with his own hand.

Deep in the bark they sunk their claws,
And at their tails began to gnaw.
After a great deal of chattering and cries of pain
Their tails were gnawed in twain.
From the loss of blood, courage they lacked
In carrying out their deadly act.

When their tails around their necks they tried to
    shift,
Behold ! they were as a rod of iron frozen stiff ;
In the tree top they could no longer cling
So they dropped below with intention to fling
Their wretched selves in the jaws of some beast of
    prey.
When a machairodus came nigh,the madam scampered
    away.

" You coward !" cried Mr. Darwin with a whine,
" You left your tail, are you blind ?
Come back, death anyhow is our lot ;
However, for the enemy I intend to make it hot."
He, brave fellow, grasped his severed tail
And with it the tiger furiously assailed.

The first blow broke its snout,
The second put an eye out,
The third put out the other eye,
And the fourth made it die.
Thus was how our ancestor, we see,
Displayed in warfare his first sagacity.

Inquired the madam, from the place of refuge to
      which she fled,
" By Jove, Charles, are you sure it is dead?
Better beat it with my tail a while.
I will remain here and on danger smile ;
Be sure you kill the great horrible brute,
From its skin why not make ourselves a suit? "

" You are good at planning, you little coward,
Though methinks your ideas most too forward ;
However, should I conclude to use the hide,
Would need it all, and, by my pride,
Which henceforth shall be my only pelf,
I declare you had better kill something for yourself."

Mr. Darwin began stripping off the skin,
And when removed he crawled in ;
He strutted about with an imperial smile
Exclaiming—" Oh my ! the weather, how mild,
I could have escaped all these years of pain
Had I only put to use my fertile brains."

This vaunting roused up the madam's wrath ;
With tail in paws she started on the war-path—
She fled down a hillside, abruptly steep,
And in the thicket discovered a musk sheep,
On seeing it was alone she began an attack;
A single blow broke the ram's back.

Another blow put the combatants at peace.
The madam began taking off the fleece,

Rather, she removed skin and all,
And into it with alacrity crawled.
Being almost starved, she appeased her appetite on
    mutton,
And ate till almost ready to burst—our first glutton.

On taking a good sleep, as naps the gastronomist,
At home from a French restaurant, where he ate of
    everything on the list,
The madam proceeded back in quest of her com-
    panion,
And was grievously surprised to find him gone.
As a memento he left behind a portion of his tail
And footprints that led across the vale.

The madam followed on in the footprints,
And where cropped out a reef of hardest flint
Came upon the object of her search,
Sitting, cross-legged like a tailor, upon a perch,
Fashioning a rude hatchet from the rock.
This was the beginning of the neoliphic epoch.

" Ho there, Charles, so you are here—I am sure
That my suit is much nicer than yours ;
And, besides, I had a first-rate meal
The best one since the dinosaur left the field.
What are you trying to do with that stone,
And what means this long-pointed bone ? "

" You ignoramus," replied the inventive genus,
"If existence is to depend on our struggles, we must
Of course have efficient weapons in order to cope
With the ox on the plain, the stag on the slope,
And, in fact, be ever ready to slay
Every beast that thwarts our way.

From one of my adversary's bones I made this dagger,
A single thrust would make a mammoth stagger ;
This (holding aloft the chipped stone) is a battle-axe,
A good one it is, though a handle it lacks.

The handle must be of something tough, like bone of
    the whale,"
Suggested the madam, "why not handle it with your
    tail?"

Hard by the reef, hollowed by ocean waves,
Was a shelf of rock, a sort of cave,—
Here for a long time a bear had dwelt,
When, finding Bruin asleep, the apes would pelt
Him with stone and other missile,
To hear him growl and to see him bristle.

Mr. Darwin, on handling the axe,
Strode forth, Bruin to attack,
With battle-axe over his shoulder—
Than he never was there a warrior bolder,
Not even Hercules when into hell groping his way,
To bring Erebus up to the light of day.

The madam followed her courageous lord close up to
    the cavern ;
Instead of finding Bruin asleep, as she had yearned,
He was in a most calefactive mood :
Few moments prior a machairodus on his premises did
    intrude.
He ousted the audacious trespasser
With few savage blows from his paws.

Courageous Mr. Darwin still strode on,
So did the madam, with courage gone,
When Bruin rose on his haunches in hostile attitude
And roared savagely, resonant became the wood.
The trembling madam gazed on a low hanging bough
And moaned, "O, Charles! if I only had my tail
    now."

"Hush," replied Mr. Darwin, with vituperous mien,
" O'er spilt milk there's no use of crying!

To such servile longings we must now be as strangers.
Fear not, I am able to surmount such danger.
When Bruin begins an attack,
Your place of safety is at my back."

"You insignificant bundle of fur," growled the bear
"Of my paw 'tis well that you beware."
Bruin extended his paw for a cuff
Which Mr. Darwin adroitly dodged.   The rebuff
Was a single sweep of the fatal axe,
Ending the tragedy in a single act.

Bruin being declared an enemy of war,
Mr. Darwin began to pillage according to law ;
The plunder consisted of a single mouldy bone,
A small quantity of berries, gathered when half-grown,
A heap of leaves that long were shed,
Twigs and bark—Bruin's bed.

As the enemy was overthrown,
They claimed the cavern as their own—
Here they lived for many years,
Subsisting upon beasts that prowled near.
This was the cradle of every nation
From out of which sprung civilization.

When the sere earth her youth renewed,
And life reigned triumphant o'er solitude,
These children of Evolution came forth ;
Their progeny scattered south and north,
Cities they built upon the plain
And chose a ruler to o'er them reign.

Such is the Evolutionist's theory !
If such be true life indeed is dreary.
Good and Evil become as the same,
Oblivion o'er the past and future will reign.
If such be the case give me the form of an ass,
That I may, like Nebuchadnezzar, subsist upon grass.

GRANDFATHER'S BOOTS.

These Boots have travelled o'er lands wide,
'Tis said they are made of a bull's hide
That fought in the Amphitheatre at Rome.
They have proven disastrous to coat-tails for genera-
    tions,
And on one occasion fatally injured a gnome.

They spoiled the swallow-tail of an English swell
Long before our Independence was born.
They have trod the heights where Warren fell,
And were on the feet of General Washington
When he crossed Delaware River with his pine gun.

They have been at the bottom of Atlantic Ocean
And were fished up when the cable was laid.
Of parting not a stitch had any notion,
In the right one was found a costly pearl
And in the left the largest toe nail in the world.

They have crossed our great Plains;
And when the party was attacked by Indians
Grandfather into one of them crawled;
The spears and arrows, though well aimed,
Proved harmless as hairpins in a lady's waterfall.

" Old Stogies " by everybody they're called,
Still they have been at many a ball;
Grandfather pronounced them a regular bore
They being so heavy that he broke through his sweet-
    heart's floor,
She, like a sensible maid, told him to come no more.

When father on earth came to dwell,
He occupied the right one for a cradle;
The boot was regularly taken to bed
And often cast at the watch-dog, 'tis said,
That howled whenever not being fed.

Once father arrayed himself in disguise with good
    intention,
And wore them to a Woman's Rights Convention;
By them his identity became known.
There were scores of shrieks and a great rustle
As he began plying them to their bustles.

They have sailed as boats on the great Lakes,
And many a cargo of boot-jacks they did take;
Once when starting from a wharf at Chicago
Into one of them crawled an intelligent editor.
Before sailing a league his pen he thrust through the
    toe.

By such harsh usage they are somewhat demolished
But still they are not aliens to boot polish.
Many boot-blacks have over them plied the brush,
They have matured and their breathing a long since
    hushed;
Man is transitory as footprints in the dust.

Many a generation they will yet serve 'tis true,
For yet they are nearly as good as new,
Save few nails are missing from the soles.
They seem everlasting, while life melts away like ice,
Some soul yet unborn will wear them on entering
    Paradise.

THE MOON IS MADE OF GREEN CHEESE.

Behold! thou radiant orb in heaven suspended,
With empyre rays thy beams hath blended.
Since the Creator bade thee to preside o'er night,
The stars to do thee homage ever take delight.
How thy lambent beams dance o'er land and seas
But thou, O moon, art made of green cheese.

When this queen of the celestial dome
In her majesty vanquishes night's gloom
What splendor to the whole universe she presents.
The diamond-eyed stars twinkle with innocence,
Each orb striving their opaque queen to please,
Despite she is made of green cheese.

And when she begins to wane
It seems as if her beauty would never return again.
Unlike a beautiful woman, when beauty is o'er
Her face attracts the entranced lover no more
But with thee, modest moon, youth and old age
    agrees,
For thou art made of green cheese.

When on us she turns her ebon back,
Enrobing the universe in a mantle black,
And we are left to grope our way in the dark,
To church, the theatre, skating-rink, the park,
Or into silent woods, and 'mid solitude these
We yearn for the moon, which is made of green
    cheese.

After a while a new moon is begot,
Which in the ethereal expanse is hardly a jot;
And as each fleeting day passes by
She increases in volume and dignity,
Till assuming her most sublime degrees
And smiles, because she is made of green cheese

Thus the moon comes and goes
Like summer showers and winter snows;
She is old as the hills, though only four weeks old,
And illumines regions both hot and cold,
Delves the glen and floats o'er seas.
Wonderful moon ! made of green cheese.

The jovial old man in this orb smiles,
Because he hath neither spouse nor child;

He meanders o'er his domains by night or day,
And exclaims—" I am monarch of all I survey !"
He laughs, scolds, and does just as he doth please,
For his whole domains are made of green cheese.

Adieu, old man, I wish thee good health,
Long life, happiness, and, above all, wealth.
Adieu, fair moon, I wish thee good-luck ;
I must cease or I will be moon-struck.
May you ever continue to enjoy luxury and ease,
And make the whole world believe you are made of
    green cheese.

APOSTROPHE TO THE SUN.

Thou glory of creation and king of the universe,
Proclaim unto man what power gave thee birth,
Why doth thou nourish our own little sphere,
While at thy control are worlds of celestial gran-
    deur?
Above and below smile stars enrolled in silvery band,
Why doth thou lend thy radiance to sustain humble
    man ?

Thou reignest uninterrupted o'er land and seas ;
Thy laughing beams dance on the gentle breeze.
How rejoiced the universe new-born
As thou rose o'er the waves on creation's morn
Behesting Darkness to yield unto Day.
And thou wert witness to the birth of man
As the Creator bade him to arise from clay.

Night's silvery 'luminator settles 'neath the western
    wave,
And the stars hide themselves after their nocturnal
    parade ;
The gnarly forest monarch matures and passes away
Even the everlasting hills crumble with decay,

The devasting haud of time engraves no furrows in
    thy brow,
Behold! with Creation's splendor thou shinest now.

Many a time thou art enrolled in a mistyshroud
And ride triumphantly 'mong tempestuous clouds,
Athwart thy radiant face the flashing fire of heaven
    plays,
And the flash of thunder frightens for a time thy
    rays.
From on high, far above the loftiest mount's crest,
Thou lookest on smiling at the tempest.

A WINTER EVE.

Close around the hearth let us gather
And heap on the fuel, for rough weather
Reigns without. Behold the trees!
How they toss and moan, as if to please
The furious winter gale
That wafts snow o'er hill and vale.

The frost on the window-pane
Hath painted many a plain
And grotesque scene. See the castle
On the crest of precipitous hill,
Through rents in the massive walls
Many a moombeam seems to crawl.

The gale moans, howls, now roars,
It hath great rage in store
To vent on some belated traveller
Out on the desolate prairie afar,
And on the poor in the large city,
Where wealth is blind to pity.

Stars in the dull cold sky
Twinkle with a dim eye
No beauty can they behold
In gazing on a land so cold,
But shed their smiling rays
On a land where reigns perpetual day.

ON COMPLETION OF MY TWENTY-FIFTH YEAR.

On this humid spring-day it is said
    That I have completed my twenty-fifth year,
And whilst this time was passing o'er my head
    Many a bright bow in the sky did appear.
The brightest one, if I remember right,
Was on the dawn of a darksome night.

And within this night my soul inquired
    For what purpose it was engendered,
On the winds that had but one retired
    To their familiar bourn. A voice was heard
Saying: "In heaven lay ye up treasures,
Vain, O vain, are worldly pleasures!"

In retrospection I'm engrossed:
    What have I accomplished in all this time?
Nothing! And youth its last charm hath lost.
    The rugged heights of manhood I must climb.
From the crest what is there for me to behold,
Nothing, save clouds, desolate and cold.

Once the dreary world was fair,
    Love and joy sprang from everything;
Till joy and love wedded misery and despair,
    And soared away on falcon-like wings,
Like the Phœnix rising from its own ashes or pell,
Leaving me alone to survey my desolate self.

I WILL PACK MY GRIPSACK.

I will pack my gripsack, and off to China I'll go,
For my lady-love has a new string to her bow.
This string is so strong that the others are all loose,
And for them she will have no further use.

One and all she will cast them away,
Where they will remain till some idle day,
Till a poor old crooked bow snaps this string in twain,
And one of them will be used again.

THE MOTHER-IN-LAW.

O, who hath not read of war, of distress,
   Of floods, of fire, of shipwreck, and famine,
   Ere a page of disaster's catalogue we examine,
We learn there is a retributive Nemesis.

Worse than the goddess of retribution,
   Is a creature that nearly every young husband pos-
      sesses,
   Who congeals him and his loving spouse's caresses;
'Tis the mother-in-law whom death shuns.

Ofttimes this marvellous creature
   Is a genuine Amazon, a Jumbo,
   And when in her awful presence we go,
We dare not look on her Medusa-like features.

Then, again, she is small and thin,
   With always abundance of brass on hand;
   Her tongue is sort of a magician's wand,
And perpetual motion is her chin.

Emphatically she makes her wants known,
  In general she raises the Old Harry.
  Ah me ! when we her daughter marry
For our folly how dearly we atone !

LIFE IS BUT AN EMPTY DREAM.

Well didst thou assert, sweet Psalmist,
  That " Life is but an empty dream,"
Hanging o'er the sea of Time, 'tis as a mist
  That disappears mysteriously as Lethe's stream.

This transitory existence designated Life,
  Which thou meted out as three-score-and-ten
      years
We live; but if all-wise Providence be rife,
  At morn we're wafted from this mutable sphere.

We dream throughout this dubious season,
  Such dreams as are empty and absurd, indeed ;
But should we, at last, recourse to reason,
  Lo ! the vineyard hath o'errun with weeds.

O then, what efforts we make,—
  The blood nearly bursts from our veins ;
But soon as we a second view take,
  We deem it, which it is, a chimeric aim.

We sink back into our familiar footsteps,
  And plod on as our sires did before us,
Knowing that ere long we must sleep as hath slept
  Our race, Death first spread his sable wings o'er us.

CALLOW YOUTH'S MUSTACHE.

When down appears on a callow youth's upper lip,
  So that it can be discerned in frosty weather,
To a tonsorial artist he goes to get it clipped,
  Squandering all the pennies he has got together.

A week passes, and, my! that mustache
  You can just behold it on closest scrutiny;
Again the artist relieves him of his cash,
  His lip from its enormous burden is free.

Another week goes by, what a change!
  The mustache's growth is truly egregious;
On Saturday eve in the shop, does it seem strange
  That we should find him soliciting trust?

The mustache is now a healthy one indeed,
  And its possessor concludes to let it grow.
As in the shade grows the weed,
  So it prospers 'neath his nose's shadow.

The mustache its possessor doth tax,
  For dyes of color, as Rising Sun Stove Polish
A brush to apply the same, and wax
  Which doth its scraggy nature abolish.

Ah, how delightful! it rises and falls
  Whenever its owner sees anything alarming;
When he on his sweetheart calls
  She declares it is "simply charming."

ONE-AND-TWENTY.

One-and-twenty to the minor sweet
Is such an age: then he looks the world
In the face, votes, pays taxes, courts his girl,
Marries her without parental consent, greets
All, save his mother-in-law, with exultation
As he is a full-fledged lord of creation.

One-and-twenty to the apprentice means liberty,
Usually freedom a suit kit of tools, a pocket full
Of his tutor's recommendations that oft pull

Him on to success.   A sheepskin to the
Young sprig of the law is his pride,
So it was with me, but I have laid it aside.

At one-and-twenty we place our shoulder
To the wheel of stern Reality, and struggle
Painfully onward.   Oft before our eyes bursts the
        bubble
Of Fortune.   Then to our father and older
Sire we go in despondence with empty purse,
And betimes he partly satisfies our avaricious thirst

At one-and-twenty we marry
('The Lord be praised if we do not),
Some pretty Miss whose mother is nought
To happiness.   She raises the Old Harry,
Turns us out of doors, diverts our happy course,
Usually ending in a decree of divorce.

At one-and-twenty we may die,—
Well, that's nothing strange, since
Flesh doth wither like leaves of the quince,
Fig, olive, and orange tree.   However, we try
To prolong life by taking prescriptions of some quack,
Who avers his skill is able to call Samuel back.

THE GREAT WONDER.

Since Philosopher Franklin flew his kite, drew
Lightning down, and Professor Morse invented tele-
        graphy,
Wonders have been accomplished by electricity.
With our cousins in Africa we can renew
Former acquaintances by sending a despatch,
And receive a reply ere eggs by steam are hatched.

Choice Havana cigars are made of cabbage leaves,
Whiskey from old boots, starch from potatoes,
Sugar from beets, Bologna sausage, that appease the
    woes
Of an empty stomach, 'tis said, of dogs. Sorely
    grieves
The belle on the death of a favorite poodle,
Or the gastronomist when scorched is his soup noodle,

For years I have seen gunpowder remain in the keg.
The sword in the scabbard, the knife in its sheath,
The revolver in its pouch, the ramrod beneath
The gun-barrel, and chickens lie down and cross their
    legs
Whenever the minister came to dine. *The Great*
    Wonder I found
Is to attend church and not see the hat passed around.

THE BARBER'S POLE.

You who have travelled the country round
    Have you not noticed the barber's pole?
The stripes begin at the top, and on reaching ground
    They encircle the sign several times,—the whole
Is a brilliant display of paint, and very few
Are of other colors except red, white, and blue.

THE SHIP OF FATE.

As the first sunbeam gilded the hill's crest
    I strolled adown the beach of an ocean,
And as I gazed o'er its fluctuating breast
    The waves were rolling with slow motion.
8

From among them rose the sun,
   And as his disc rested on the brine,
O'er the meads his beams began to run
   Embalming all in glad sunshine.

Fresh was the breeze from off the sea
   And uncommonly sweet the birds' carol,
Gray and mossy were the rocks, green the trees,
   'Mong them a crystal brooklet did purl.

There was but one sail in sight,
   Well-fashioned with masts tall,
As she sped on her broad wings white,
   To her, methought, no disaster could befall.

From the mast-head streamed a pennon
   And from astern her country's flag,
As she through the brine did run
   Slightly to one side she sagged.

Many a bubble receded in her wake
   And after a moment they would burst,
Like all our joys when we attempt to slake
   From the fount of Happiness our thirst.

Proudly her commander trod the deck
   As the meridian of Youth was he ;
His countenance wore a serious aspect,
   Yet I heard him laugh with glee.

Those obedient to his command
   Were, I deem, of still fewer years,
Not one of this juvenile band
   Seemed brawny enough to be here.

I gazed on each fair young face
   And nought was there, I opine,
That would cause joyance to waste
   As to frosts doth the eglantine.

And whilst gazing on their craft
  The sky became o'ercast with clouds,
A sudden gust began to waft
  O'er shoals furious waves that roared loud.

The sails were quickly furled,
  On came the vehement blast ;
On beam's end she was hurled
  And uprighted with a broken mast.

The commander—a few minutes ago a youth,
  Was now a man of proud mien ;
The mates, pilot, and whole crew, in sooth,
  Were stalwart men as ever seen.

How battled the noble craft with the waves !
  It seemed as if she must go down
Unmourned, unshrouded, to that grave
  Where fleets of every nation are found.

The gale increased its rage,
  What words can depict this storm ?
The mariner's faces were now wan with age,
  Bent and withered were their stalwart forms.

The commander, lashed to a broken spar,
  Gave orders in slow and labored speech ;
At the wheel two gray-haired tars,
  The mercy of the Lord did beseech.

They cut away mast and spars,
  And were drifting a hopeless wreck ;
Lashed fast was many a tar,
  Yet the waves swept them from the deck.

The storm had now somewhat abated,
  But their love of life was nearly run ;
Not a single soul was elated
  On catching a gleam of the setting sun.

In a goodly harbor they were secure,
　But their career was defunct;
And in the early twilight pure,
　'Neath the waves they sunk.

They sunk, as we all must sink,
　'Neath the overwhelming flood of years,
Where forgetfulness forges links
　Of our virtues, faults, aspirations and fears.

MAN'S MISFORTUNE.

There was a time in long bygone days,
　When man from toil was free ;
In Indolence's ambrosial rays
　He stretched himself at ease.

Each tree yielded delicious fruit,
　Nectar gushed in every rill ;
Not a care did Necessity refute,
　All ate and drank their fill.

The dark, gloomy prison was unbuilt,
　Unforged was the shackle and chain;
The felon never expiated his guilt,
　And no martyr was ever consumed by flames.

Disease came not to torture the soul,
　And Death never claimed the young ;
In dreamless slumber passed away the old,
　While in their ears soothing songs were sung.

Oft 'mid evergreen bowers,
　In some cool, shady grove,
Man passed many a happy hour
　Under the smiles of Jove.

Some who delighted to roam
　Where fancy might please,
Steered their crafts 'mid foam,
　And sailed o'er coral seas.

There were no treacherous shoals,
　From which the Siren sang her song;
Mars claimed not a soul,
　For no tempest raged strong.

The ocean, land and sky
　Was ever tranquil, beautiful, serene;
Just as we shall behold on high,
　After cold, mute death intervenes.

Ah! such was the Golden Age,
　From earth forever gone;
From the Book of Life a page
　Of bliss beyond comprehension.

It fled when Pandora ope'd her box,
　From out of which flew Disease and Woe,
To fall upon the young and the old with hoary
　locks,
　To all mankind she was a foe.

She called lightning down from the sky,
　Where wild tempests loudly roar;
She bade Æolus pile the waves on high
　And strew wrecks along the shore.

She sent envy among the human race,
　With those she was at all pleased;
Exalted them to a high place
　For their kin to cry, "O Your Royal Majesty!"

" O your Royal Highness,"
　Resounds the cry from across the sea
Where millions toil on in distress,
Scourged by ignorance and poverty.

THE FATE OF A YELLOW-LEGGED ROOSTER.

A Plymouth Rock rooster, with yellow legs,
    Mounted the coop, loud rang his clarion.
The many a setting hen on her eggs
    Awoke to greet the tranquil morn.

" Why do you make such a noise ? " hissed a drake,
    On taking his head from under his wing ;
" If I such an uproar did make
    I hope somebody would my neck wring."

For reply the rooster crowed still louder,
    Which set both drake and ducks a-hissing ;
The noise was like the burning of loose powder
    Or a score of young ladies a-kissing.

" Hush up ! " squawked a monstrous gander,
    Ruler of a numerous flock of geese,
" With such a pest in our coop 'tis no wonder
    That we never enjoy a moment's peace."

The rooster crowed again, the geese hissed
    And in wrath waddled to the brook ;
Their sumptuous breakfast they missed ;
    The first time since from the shell they looked.

" Let us drown the nuisance," said a goose,
    As she floated past the gander ;
To our master he's no earthly use
    And each day tries to excel in egotistic grandeur.

" No," quoth a wise gosling—" but let us 'mong the
        rushes hide,
    For to-day the minister comes to dine ;
From the mark I will not come wide
    That he will suit the appetite of the divine,"

"Agreed," hissed the flock in a homogeneous hiss,
  Which at length ended in sonorous tones;
Ere the sun goes down we wist
  That the divine will pick his bones."

The sun rose high, the geese sought a shady bower
  'Neath some o'erhanging brush;
And all exulting when in that fatal hour
  His blood from every vein would gush.

Again sounded the crowing ending in a squawk.
  A flutter and nothing more was heard
Save the cries of a fish-hawk
  And the chirp of some miniature birds.

At eve when they returned, O what a sight!
  A familiar head sodered in the sun,
Some feathers, and two yellow legs bright
  Attested the rooster's race was run.

"BABY MINE."

My sorrow began the other morn,
  And O, how can I bear it!
The dear babe is gone
  And his crib is up in the garret.

Never more will he crow
  On taking a dose of soothing syrup,
Or his hand try to swallow
  With mouth open wide as a stirrup.

He was ruler of the house and all
  In which he was the hero;
And on his pa he would call
  For hash, sausage, and potato.

The Angel of Death took him one night
  And O, what sadness filled my heart !
After the spirit had taken flight
  With the clay I could hardly part.

THE FROG AND TURTLE.

Jerry Butler was as fat a frog
As ever croaked from the fogs ;
Of a pond in New England ;
Where marshes and tracts of sand
Constitute nearly the whole surface.
Here the farmer on his barren waste
Cultivates corn for his succotash
And from 'neath the waves that clash
Upon the rock-bound coast clams he takes,
And participates in a clam bake.

" Ah," croaked Jerry as he mounted a log,
" In all New England I'm the finest frog ;
Just see me now !   My legs
Are as fat as butter in the keg.
My skin like silverware shines ;
When the king in his hall comes to dine,
Wouldn't I make a splendid dish ?
I would gratify any Frenchman's wish ;
But I am far too crafty a fellow
By such a fiend to be laid low ;
He has taken so many of my kin
That our population is very thin.
Often he strove to capture me
Ah, Ah, I were too crafty.
Ere this he must have concluded
That I cannot be taken by lead,
Spear, hook, or any other device
That has so many of my kin to destruction enticed."

" Has the fiend gone yet ? " inquired a turtle,
Thrusting his ugly head from the shell
And scrutinizing every nook and corner keen,
To ascertain the whereabouts of the " fiend "
(A Yankee in quest of turtles for soup).
Upon a snag 'neath a willow that o'er the pond
  drooped
Climbed the turtle. Thus to the frog it began.
" It seems to me, if I were you, to scan
The danger you are subjected to,
I would not sit there in full view.
The enemy may be close at hand,
And ere the peril you could understand
A simple discharge from his fatal gun
You would receive.   Your race would be run.
To sit there is equivalent to self-slaughter;
Why not seek safety 'neath the water ? "

Replied Jerry, swelling like a bubble,
" Pshaw ! don't fret, you're always borrowing trouble.
If I possessed your horny back,
I would defy the whole human pack.
Like Juno's crab biting at Hercules' heel,
So would I on the enemy steal,
Fasten my jaws on some vital part,
Showing that I too could play the destructive art.
And, as he turned to flee,
I would mount his back
Like the old man of the sea.
At his nose I would hew and hack
Till it was all worn away.
Then hold of an ear I would lay,
More savage than a dog biting at a swine's.
When in pain he began to whine
I would tell him to hold his breath
In order to howl on the approach of death."
" Silence, the enemy is coming," snapped the turtle,
" He is crouched 'neath yon myrtle ;
Anyhow I shall keep out of sight."

The turtle dove with all its might,
The ripples from the splash
In the bright sunshine flashed.
Jerry began to croak very loud,
Of his voice he was proud.
Suddenly there came a loud report,
And Jerry's life was cut short.

COMPOSED ON RETURNING FROM A DANCING PARTY.

'Tis midnight's silent hour,
　And I have just returned from the party.
There mirth with its hilarious power,
　Bestowed a special favor on me.
The gloom that o'erspreads my mind
Was for a brief duration left behind.

O blissful mirth, come again !
　O music so soft and sweet,
To thy voluptuous strains
　Flew many light feet.
Ah, thou art a heavenly boon,
Even when sounding in the ball-room.

There I met a winsome lady ;
　She was beautiful, angelic ;
In each gesture her soul did lay,
　And her laughter was the wick
On which the flame, amiability, fed.
Alas ! she was already wed.

O lady, in thy dark eyes,
　. Many attractions I did discern ;
High in my bosom my heart did rise.
　The flame of adoration began to burn,
But I extinguished it for aye
Ere my tongue a word did say.

TO-DAY, DAD, I AM OF AGE.

Ah! Ah! to-day, Dad, I am of age.
No longer to roost in the parental cage,
Or to get up mornings on the break of day
To kindle fires, from door-steps to brush the snow
      away;
Nor go to the barn to feed the horses, milk the cows,
Let out the calves, swill the old sow,
And do up all the other chores,
While you, Dad, lie a-bed and snore.

For my services, I shall now demand compensation
And spend my money on marbles or fun.
Often on you, Dad, I shall call for cash
To pay the tonsorial artist for dyeing my mustache,
Cutting my hair, shaving me on the chin
To make the beard grow ('tis dreadfully thin),
Though some day, Dad, I am very sure,
I shall have a beard that will excel yours.

I think I might as well begin to read law,
And in the neighborhood mend each flaw.
Of course I intend to charge a handsome fee.
When a client in trouble comes to me,
I shall make him believe that revenge is sweet as
      honey
(Which it really is), and when I get all his money,
Should he insinuate I am unjust,
I shall just tell him to go to Erebus.

TO A SILK HAT.

O hat! when on this empty head of mine
Thou doth make each thought wholly **divine** ;
The defective world seems integral,
And ant-hills into mountains swell.

The stagnant pond from which bullfrogs sing
Grows cool and clear as the Helicon spring;
The jay, loon, duck, goose, and prairie hen carol
Sweetly as the canary in its cage on the wall.

The grasshopper and ant dance a jig
To the grunting of the Guinea pig;
Faithful Pegasus canters with his rider
On eating red pepper and drinking hard cider.

The cows from the pasture low,
Because the moon has melted all the snow;
Fishes swim to some arid height
And watch the morning-glory open at night.

The sun requests the man in the moon
To sing and harp his liveliest tune;
The stars cling to a comet's tail,
The rapid flight makes them pale.

The gnome comes from the bosom of the earth
To show the beggar what he is worth;
Orpheus descends with his harp into hell,
And brings back the one he loves so well.

Cerebus has become a shaggy poodle,
And is asleep in the lap of a noodle;
Wonder upon wonders I hear of and see
Because thou, a hat, solves all mystery.

In thy upper story lies the magician's wand,
The philosopher's stone is hidden 'neath thy band;
I must put thee away (though for ye I thirst),
Or thou wilt surely cause my head to burst.

ON BEHOLDING THE SUN SET.

The sun is low in western cadence,
  The levant horizon in golden splendor is o'ercast,
Another day hath gone whence
  It becomes an atom of the past,
And with it also went
Many a gem-studded moment.

Within this short period of sunlight
  What wonders were engendered ;
Pleasures were pursued that excite
  The soul. Groans, too, were heard
Which came from every hand,—
Groans and tears fill our land.

O the words, though idly spoken,
  Hath caused many a heart to break ;
And hearts that at dawn were broken
  Now cease to beat, and they take
Their final rest in the bosom of the earth,
While the censorious lips ring with mirth.

The moon comes o'er the eastern hills
  With her fair face partly veiled in clouds,
Her soft beams flow in limpid rills
  Across broad fields and forests proud.
Upon the lake's bosom see her lambent shadows,
And how the phosphorescent wavelets glow!

Could I but construct a substantial bark
  From these pellucid beams, and sail o'er
Some tranquil sea where no dark
  Storms ever rage, where the shore
Is never strewn with wrecks, I am sure
That from these shortcomings I would be secure.

The stars come forth, and there are none
  In the whole firmament that are dilatory
In expressing gratitude in their bright twinkling tone ;
  And all shine forth with resplendent glory,
Bidding mortal no longer 'mid doubt to grope,
But to look above where reigns, triumphant, Hope.

This is Night, the season in which Nature rests,
  And on gazing into her half-closed eyes
What beauty is revealed.   In quest
  Of true sublimity we need not further scrutinize ;
Here is an unpenned volume of profound lore
Of mysteries present and of those gone before.

POOR AVIS.

Come, John, let's view the spot
  Whereon we used to play,
Beside the crumbling cot
  Of good old neighbor Gray.

The fence is razed to the ground,
  The gate, too, has fallen in decay,
And not a fragment can be found
  Of that tree 'neath which we used to play.

The spring at the foot of the hill,
  Whereat we often quenched our thirst, is dry ;
But that pine stands there still,
  With gigantic trunk towering high.

The hill is not quite so steep
  Adown which we used to coast,
The wind as it o'er the crest sweeps
  Howls as shrieks a ghost.

The grove whose boughs to the breeze waved
  By a forest fire was long laid low,
And all is silent as the grave
  Or the Northland of ice and snow.

Alas! sweet Avis is gone,
  She married an auctioneer;
John, do you remember the morn
  That I forbid you to see her?

Yes, John, 'twas foolish in me,
  She had completely won my heart;
And life was full of monotony
  When from her I was apart.

Ah! those happy hours that she and I together passed,
  Their remembrance brings forth a tear;
But our fondest hopes are sure to blast
  As Winter is cold and drear.

When blasted are our hopes
  For mortal what remains?
'Tis but to grieve, as we grope
  Through Life's mysterious domains.

The worthless scamp she married,
  (For many good reasons I never did admire),
There was nothing in his empty head,
  His tongue would perpetual motion tire.

What it was that took her eye
  I have never been able to explain;
He possessed neither wealth nor dignity,
  But wore a silk hat and swung a cane.

He made her believe he had wealth in plentitude
  Though he wasn't worth a shilling;
Really, he was not a fourth-rate dude.
  To marry a dude, girls are usually willing,

How oft they scorn an honest mechanic,
   Who by the sweat of the brow earns his bread ;
Even at the sight of him they grow sick,
   As if he were some monster to dread.

Well, after they got married,
   They went on their wedding tour
To Delhi, some four miles ahead,
   A hamlet dismal and sour.

Here they stopped to admire the scenes,
   And partook of their wedding dinner :
Of two crackers, a plate of Boston-baked beans,
   And a pickle that would ire a sinner.

Over such a meal poor Avis cried,
   Declaring she deserved something better,
He rose to the acme of his pride
   And vowed an oyster-stew he would get her.

For a single dish of oysters he called,
   And at the delinquent waiter he began to hoot
And as the waiter entered the dining hall,
   Said he would take five cents worth of the soup.

He opened his purse—it contained not a nickel,
   But a quid of tobacco and a brass collar-button,
Still he was unabashed in such a pickle ;
   And devoured the whole stew like a glutton.

Poor Avis bit her lips, she was much abashed,
   And began to seriously upbraid him ;
He, the worthless scamp, stroked his dyed mous-
    tache
And smiled—nothing dismayed him.

Said he at length—"Waiter, I will let you under-
    stand
   That I possessed wealth till the bank broke,
Then every dollar disappeared like land
   When a north sea dyke has broke.

There's a time close at hand,
  When I can purchase this whole town
Many servants will be at my command,
  Few of whom on me now frown."

Such was the scamp poor Avis wed,
  Instead of loving him, she did fear;
Her offspring number a dozen head,
  Nine of them are auctioneers.

RIVER OF DEATH.

O River of Death—O River of Death,
  O'er thy dark upheaving bosom,
Our loved ones are borne, and left
  Upon that shore, mysteriously dumb.

Ever and anon we hear the splash,
  As ye surge against thy sable shore,
And as ye adown rapids dash,
  We tremble at the awful roar.

Laboriously across thy breast,
  The boatman, with age hoary,
Proceeds—a harbinger of rest,
  And he bears the weary to glory.

There is rest beyond thy sable shore,
  Where the tree of life ne'er blights,
And there with saints we shall adore,
  The Author of our immortal light.

A day, a week, a month, or a year,
  Will have wrought no change on our brow,
The eye will ne'er be charged with tears,
  Nor the heart break as it doth now.
9

Those we loved here below,
  And gave up so reluctantly,
Will meet us with countenance aglow,
  As we enter the realm of eternal Day.

Beyond thy ebon shore no tears are there
  An exotic guest is the broken heart,
No ear hears a groan of despair,
  Sin hurls not its fatal darts.

I yearn at times to see thy seething billows,
  And to behold the boatman old,
For the loss of a loved one I wear the willow,
  Who long ago crossed thy bosom cold.

Death took my brother—a playmate,
  When his life was yet at dawn,
And I am spared by the fates,
  Who left me here to mourn.

Death is mortal's inevitable end,
  As thou, O river, doth see,
Life is but a brook that wends
  Its way to the ocean of eternity.

So long as man on earth appears,
  Thou, O river, will sorrow behold,
A flood of human tears,
  Broken hearts and ruined souls.

IN THE PROSPECT OF DEATH.

The Power, poor soul, that gave thee birth,
  Will soon call thee from out thy carnate abode,
No more to be a transitory tenant of earth,
  Encumbered with sin's oppressive load.

The few brief years thou wert here,
  Thou didst battle 'gainst odds, incessantly,
Groaned at thy own wretchedness, shed tears,
  And in vain looked for the dawn of a brighter
    day.

Thou wert familiar with life in all its woes;
  By the hand of Despair thou wert fed,
Quaffed gall from Friendship's goblet, and God
    knows,
  That from many an immaculate wound thou bled.

The brief spell thou hath yet to spend,
  Direct thy attention to the Power,
Which by its grace alone can defend,
  Thee from destruction in so dark an hour,

And now, before Repentance's throne,
  Confess all thy faults and sins,—
By so doing thou wilt surely atone,
  For them all and heaven win.

For thee there's an abode in heaven,
  When Empyrea sheds its doric rays
Over saints who on earth were forgiven,
  And by faith entered into eternal joy.

Though thy race is nearly run,
  The world beckons thee to return,
Promising years of joy, whose sun,
  From Sorrow's sky, all clouds burns.

Yet, it is hard indeed, O Christ,
  To relinquish the ghost so young,
But thou didst satisfy death's price
  As thou from the cross hung.

If thou wilt receive this soul of mine,
  Which is hardly acquainted with one good deed,
It will, throughout eternity's time,
  At thy feet for mercy plead.

No longer I shudder at the thought
   Of laying this erring form to rest,
For thou, O Lord, by example taught
   'Tis but a journey to the realm of the blest.

Welcome Death! I fear thee not,
   Though once a rabid virus—a terror,
To win thee, O Christ, hath been my lot,
   I err not in this hour of error.

Ah, my soul, thou art rich indeed,
   Wealthier than any gift that Mammon can give.
No more wilt thou groan and bleed,
   With crowned saints thou shalt forever live.

COMPOSED IN A BALL-ROOM.

Long it has been, Terpsichore,
   Since thou bade me be gay;
The burden of sadness that long I bore,
   A moment ago I cast away.

How the music's voluptuous strains
   Exhilarates the souls of all;
Hilarity each heart claims
   Within this capacious hall.

In the music there's a lull,
   And the busy feet are still:
These midnight moments are not dull,
   For joyance flows in rills.

The music sounds again,
   And feet are flying fast,
As if striving those moments to win
   That are gone for aye—alas!

"There is a time to dance,"
  Proclaimed the Preacher of yore;
But the Orthodox doth glance
  With contempt on the Terpsichore.

Let the growling Orthodox rail
  At so innocent a revery;
But what would life avail,
  Were it not for such a glee?

O, sound the piano and violin,
  Let strains be loud and fast;
Let smiles and laughter mingle with the din,
  For soon this season of mirth will pass.

When the time comes for me to mourn,
  I can lament with heavier heart
Than he to sober life is born
  Untaught in Joyance's many arts.

HARTWICK.

'Mong all the scenes of the West,
The one that I love best
Are those crumbling structures of brick,
The half-in-ruin village—Hartwick.

The iron bridge has fallen, the stone mill,
With its many noisy wheels, is still,
The log-dam over which the water flowed
Rotted away many years ago.

Unencumbered flows the river,
Rushing onward the same as ever;
The banks are grass-grown,
And with rubbish widely strewn.

Just as high tower the rugged hills,
On them the morning sun smiles still;
But the forest trees are gone,—
By the woodman's axe they were shorn.

At the stone quarry and brick-yard
Industry's voice no more is heard;
Over each lofty trees cast their shadow,
And tall, rank grasses grow.

The yard where repose the dead,
By drowsy negligence is neglected;
The marble slabs are broken and defaced,
Time will soon lay them all in waste.

No kind hand ever plants a flower
To beautify this long neglected bower;
Not a friend comes to mourn
Our loved ones from us forever gone.

Here, in solitude, let them dwell,
For their rest is integral;
Not for worldly fame do they pant,
They have eaten of the Lotus plant.

At the tavern no more halts the traveller,
On his way to the west afar;
No more he and his comrades applaud
Those marvellous stories of the landlord.

The numerous guests have departed,
And the silent bar-room seems sad-hearted,
For here the joker cracked his jokes,
And drank the health of many folks.

The numerous stores have dwindled down to one,
It may close its doors for aye by the set of sun;
Factories, shops, warehouses are gone,
And their fragments strew the lawn.

Mansion and cottage to the ground are razed,
And in their spacious yards cattle graze ;
Numerous swine at liberty run
Through the corridors of the prison.

The owl in the old mill's gable
Has a home, and in the night sable
It comes forth and dismally hoots
Till morn puts on its rosy suit.

In the public square still stands the liberty-pole,
Lone as a single iceberg in regions cold,
For years the flag has not floated from its head,
Surely the goddess of Liberty must be dead !

Half-way up the woodcock has built her nest
Where she finds ever welcome rest ;
The mischievous boy dare not an ascension make
For fear the pole might break.

The old church with its cracked bell,
Whose claritude once on the breeze swelled,
Ere long must crumble to the ground,—
The wind has blown the steeple down.

Where now are the numerous souls
That so often crossed the threshold?
Those having their race run,
Of their whereabouts ask the sexton.

The sexton alone seems invulnerable :
With lusty arm he still rings the bell,
The stranger he politely seats,
If one the house of worship greets.

Here the aged pastor instructs his little flock
How to build their house on Salvation's rock ;
Danger or destruction is on every hand
For hill, glen and vale are of sinking sand.

The building where school is still held
Against devastating Time has long rebelled;
Year after year continues the war,
But Time will inevitably conquer.

O Hartwick! when my weary feet
Trod many a foreign street,
How I yearned for the time to come
When I could once more behold you shimmering in
    the sun.

At last I have returned, but ah! how changed,
The once familiar objects are all estranged,
The very roof 'neath which I used to play
Years ago crumbled into decay.

Familiar faces greet me no more,
And I am disconsolate as on a foreign shore,
Where is spoken a strange language,
Each word seeming charged with rage.

Changed are the everlasting hills,
And gazing on them I am chilled,
For I deemed these rugged heights sublime
Inaccessible to the foot of Time.

Time, unshod, treads the roughest place;
Over thorny paths and over deep chasms he hastes,
But rouses not the sluggard from repose
Till his earthly career is at a close.

Ah, I have yet a friend—the river,
Whose broad surface is familiar as ever,
But where it used to surge and roar
Its angry voice is heard no more.

Like man condemned to servile penitude,
So it revolved the mill-wheels rude,
And when the day of freedom dawned
It flowed quietly—tranquil as early morn.

THE SKATING RINK.

Behold! what a deuced invention!
Something new occurs from sun to sun,
But this I declare excels all !
A miniature skating-park within walls,
And skates with wooden wheels,
Four at the toe, the same at the heel,
Fastened on the foot like any other skate,
And as ready to cause the skater to meet his fate.
Let me see: the hard maplewood floor
With chalk is often sprinkled o'er
So that the skater will not slip
Which might cause his pants to rip;
And should he chance to fall
He might receive a broken neck—that's all.
Ah, see that maid fleet on skates,
Looking over her shoulder for a mate ;
Here he comes, great awkward fellow !
He stumbles and over he goes
Both flat on the dusty floor lie,
And the many skaters circle by.
Perchance they nod or smile,—
Such mishaps occur all the while.
The couple are on their feet again
And join the circling train.
No worse off are they for the mishap,
Save his coat received a gap.
Youth and maid skate together
With perspiring brow as in warm weather.
A morose old bachelor, without a soul,
All by his sweet self around the rink rolls ;
With contempt he gazes on each maid,
Who on the arm of the youth is weighed.
Let us not forget, when he used to court
There was not this merry sport.
A young widow, gayest of the gay,
With a timid maid takes her way,
And, ere the rink is skated round,

A new companion she has found
In the person of a wedded man,
Whose anxious spouse cannot understand
Why her lord does not come to tea.
In the darkness she gazes with anxiety.
A mamma leading a four-year-old child,
On skates is learning it the style
Of skating, even if ice be out of season,
And season out of reason.
A clumsy fellow collides with a lady;
They fall, and the deal is to pay.
She denounces him in strong language,
How vehement is her temper's rage !
She cries not because she is hurt,
But over the rent in her skirt,
Which is half rent in twain,
And with tobacco spittle badly stained.
The gentlemen heed not the notice on the wall,
That they mustn't smoke or chew at all.

EUTHANASIA.

There shall come a time, and no one knows
When, these poor forms of ours will quake
At the awful sight of Mors—the foe
Of every creature that God did create.

He created man to survive the wreck of Time,
As in the Golden Age from toil and pain to be free ;
But through sin we fell, as mitigation of the crime,
He gave unto few a painless boon—thou, Euthanasia.

When inexorable Mors doth visit me,
Which may be on the morrow,
Let not a single relation bend his knee,
Nor for a moment bow his head in sorrow.

In this hour let none gather round my couch,
Nor shed friendship's collusive tear.
In words of sorrow let no tongue vouch
That my obit makes a single soul drear.

O Mors, at thy command we sink into the tomb,
This edict the mightiest of earth must obey,
And when ye pass on me my doom,
I will solicit no other favor than Euthanasia.

TRANSITORY LIFE.

" The day of one's death is far better than his birth,"
    Exclaimed the Preacher schooled in Christian love.
His wide experience here on earth
    Taught him that life is unworthy to adore.

Man that is born of woman is of few years,
    His pathway is hedged with thorns,
And his manna is his own tears,
    His hearth a shrine at which he mourns.

In the morn he groweth up like the grass,
    And before sultry noon-day is cut down;
His most benevolent deeds into an echo pass,
    And 'mong Oblivion's hills it only resounds.

The pale moonbeams, the bright sun's rays,
    When storm-clouds partly obscure the sky
Are not more uncertain than our days,
    Like the narcissus we droop and die.

In vain we strive to prolong our days
    In seeking some avenue of escape from disease
But the will of the Fates we must obey,
    Though our bark hath just entered upon tranquil
        seas.

O God! from thee each breath we borrow ;
 We are feeble as the worm in the dust,
Our existence is one of toil, pain and sorrow,
 Encumbered with disappointments and distrust.

THE BEAUTIFUL WORLD.

I yearn not for the wings of a dove
 To bear my soul from earth away,
Sacred are the things I love
 'Mong which I would like to dwell for aye.

O whisper not in fervent prayer,
 To Him who rules on high,
That this-life is full of care,
 That no pleasure in our path doth lie.

There is beauty in everything :
 There is beauty in the tempest,
There is beauty in the vivid lightning,
 And the gales that blow from out the west.

O, see ye not these green fields,
 Hear ye not those birds' songs,
And happy childhood's gladsome peals,
 As the children in the meadow pass along?

Behold this dense forest of waving trees,
 All clothed in greenest leaves,
The reaper's song is borne on the breeze
 As he binds the golden sheaves.

The cricket chirps blithe from the grass,
 The beetle rises on buzzing wings,
The shadows of objects lengthen fast,
 The philomel its evening carol sings.

The day hath gone—'tis evening now,
　The harvesters quit the field,
From the pasture come the cows,
　With the milkmaid at their heels.

No, this is not a world of pain,
　This is not a world of strife;
The whole universe attests so plain
　That joy and happiness constitute life. 　.

CONTRADICTORY LIFE.

Life in each vicissitude seems contrary
To the design of Providence.　No matter
What may be our intentions, we pay
The most severe forfeit at the
Goal of Disobedience.　Oft when life is sweetest
We're cut down or tortured with dire distress.

Here we pause to estimate life's worth
Of only few days, weeks, months, or years;
A conglomeration of hope, and disappointment, and
　　mirth
Is but the forerunner of tears,
Which to the soul is a natal boon,
An echo from the tomb.

Like a delicious fruit tree in full blossom,
Promising to bring forth abundance of fruit,
The bud is blighted by chilly winds that come
In all their severity ; such is life, and it refutes
But few withered deeds for harvest,
And of time 'tis oft a dreary waste.

While animated with this spark of celestial fire,
We should improve each talent given us;
And, when our pilgrimage on earth expires,
That which is immortal ascend it must
Into the boundaries of the spirit-land,—that which is
　　mortal
Will return to earth, whereon we dwell.

PARENTAL AFFECTION.

Delighted are parents with their new-born,
Tenderly each day they watch its growth,
When its mind expands to notice objects that adorn
The nursery, 'tis filled with wonder.   In truth
It examines the various objects round,
And in each something interesting is found.

This boon, such as parental affection alone is,
Wanes not as years go by ; and in
Long hours of sickness they tenderly watch o'er this
Pain-partaking-of child—a child of sin
And by its parents original sinful condition,
Doth it to the civil power bow in submission ?

MY UNREALIZED IDEAL.

Her beauty is without parallel,
More beautiful is she than a prize
Painting of winged habitants of the skies.
Her raven tresses in ringlets fall
Below her slender waist;
In a Cinderella-like-slipper her foot is encased.

Her eyes are of dark lustre,
O'ershadowed by long, silken lashes,
That rise and lower, as fall dashes
Of sunshine on a semi-cloudy day, which insures
Not the traveller against inclement weather.
Nor the dove cooing from the heather.

Her lips are red as wine fresh from the vintage,
Between them gleam two rows of pearly teeth,
Not wrought by the dentist; a wreath
Of seventeen summers crowns her age;
Pure heaven engendered womanhood,
Is the pedestal on which she has lately stood.

Flush as autumn sunset are her cheeks,
Through them blue veins course their way,
And at each emotion the vital tide doth lay
Itself out in bold relief.   Plainly bespeaks
Innocence through her blushes,
Pure as the river that through heaven gushes.

Her nose, rather short, is not at all puggy,
Nor does it turn up at trifles,
Like that of a society pet's, as if she smells
Odors we dislike.   An infant in its buggy
Is not more 'cute than she.   Sweet is a whiff
Of Hoyt's German Cologne on her handkerchief.

From her ears hang no useless ornaments,
Such as odd-shaped pieces of brass, gold-plated,
Or diamonds that flash as if created
In the bosom of mother earth.   The extent
Of such gems are limited, and dearly we pay
For those made of paste, or from Alaska.

Her brow high, and intelligent
Is overhung with superfine bangs,
All in little ringlets, as hangs
An artificial set o'er the brow of a parlor-pent,
Dime-novel-reading beauty.   Her brow of such a
      mold
Seems too noble for this existence brief and cold.

I love to gaze on such perfection,
Such as nature ne'er before to mortal gave--
More perfect than Powers Greek Slave.
Nowhere I am positive, under the sun,
Though on countless millions he doth shine
Is there another such a being integrally divine.

Many a time she receives visits from Adam Forepaugh,
Who urges her to accompany his wonderful circus
As the most beautiful female of America.   This place
      of trust

And envy she declines.   Ten thousand dollars fails to
   draw
Her on.   The throne of sensibility she did mount
In refusing a penniless Italian Count.

With such manifold charms attached to her
She draws more attention than an elephant walking
Through our streets, monkeys grinning, a clown
   talking.
Wherever she goes, like Mrs. Langtry, she creates a
   stir—
Never failing to enamour all she meets,
Though she possesses not Mrs. Langtry's big feet.

HAPPY SHEPHERD.

Happy shepherd, yours is a pleasant duty,
   Betimes you must be somewhat lonely;
   Is this not when all flowers are faded—only
A withered stem to mark their former beauty?
Is it not consoling to wander in the wood and mourn
O'er bright-hued treasures forever gone?

When the forest is tinged yellow
   And Autumn winds waft the golden ornaments
   To the ground, are you not troubled—giving vent
To your emotion through tears?   I know
That you, like myself, have experienced this pain.
But all will be beautiful when 'tis spring again.

How oft have you in happy days
   Strolled o'er your favorite meads, carpeted with
      flowers,
   Thence to some cool, delightful bower
   Where you poured forth in sweetest lays
The joy of your happy life
In which no care is rife.

THE ALMANAC,

That indispensable, though oft misused, pamphlet,
   The Almanac, I have perused diligently and great
To my satisfaction. There seems no limit
   To information, and specially of date
Concerning birth and death of noted personages,
     also of events
That have occurred since Nimrod first pitched his
     tent.

O pamphlet so degraded and misapplied!
   The barber uses you to wipe his razor on;
The janitor tears you asunder when his undried
   Kindlings fail to ignite. The gazer on
Your pages beholds many a wonderful thing
That nearly deprives Death of its sting.—

By this I mean discoveries in medicine.
   Why, reader, if you happen to lose an arm, all you
Would have to do is to apply a liniment thin
   To the stump, and in a week or two
A new arm will grow out as natural
As a boy takes to the bat and ball.

MY WANT.

What I want is something new,
   And this something I know not how .
To discover. Many common theme 'tis true
   I have harped and scraped upon, till now
I am left with a worn vocabulary
So exhausted that it contains nothing merry.

One cyclopedia after another I searched
   But found nothing very remarkable therein;
On the lofty pinnacle of Science I perched
   Meditated a while, but failed to win

My desideratum; thence to Washington's Biography,
And at last to Josh Billings' poor orthography.

I read his productions, but not in vain
    I learn he won popularity by spelling
Words as they sound, rendering them so plain
    They can be pronounced by a child telling
Its lesson from a primer, but his experiment
Is about as profitable as the Revised New Testament.

POST-MORTEM HONOR.

Man's good qualities are generally overlooked
    Till his Master comes as a thief in the night,
Calling on him to render account of himself, fully
        booked
    By angels duly qualified.   After the immortal light
To that mortal unexplored land takes its way
Friends assemble with tongue attuned to Eulogy.

The undertaker comes; crape is displayed in profu-
        sion,
    Clothes are brushed—some dyed jet black,
Tears flow—many are shed by collusion.
    The weeping minister eulogistically unsacks
The virtues of the deceased, who when alive
Where he kept them no one can contrive.

    When he is laid to rest—a fate
We all must sooner or later meet—
    The marble worker in exquisite state
Hews from his block, black as concrete,
    Or white as seafoam, a tombstone
Which ere long doth an inscription own.

This inscription is of virtues well distilled—
    It may be in verse or in prose
Like those on the Pilgrim headstones at Burial Hill;

Or the same as a Norther gave to those
Who, through battle, sleep 'neath southern skies,
Close to " where old Fort Pulaska lies."

Several years ago, I remember of attending
   The funeral of a brilliant attorney who,
While in full vigor, was often sending
   His fellow attorneys to despondence by logic, though
By the whole fraternity he was hated,
For in logic and wit he was unmated.

After he had passed away, the Bar met and adopted
   A series of resolutions, some in behalf
Of his services to the State, and they pleaded
   Many pathetic ones to his widow, whose staff
Of support and comfort was broken. Is it funny
They gave her sympathy instead of money?

HUMAN LIFE.

'Tis, as we all know, an old story,
   One that had its origin in the long ago,
That Human Life takes its way
   The same as rivers flow.

Those poets whose songs can never die
   Transport us to a lofty mount,
Where eternal snows coruscate on high
   Out of which gushes a crystal fount.

From this fount a streamlet proceeds,
   Babbling and pushing its way along
Till reaching broad meads,
   Then it flows wide and strong.

The verdant meads are passed,
   And a cataract appears ;
Its bosom with foam is o'ercast,
   Adown the precipice it careers.

It flows on with sullen ebb,
    And is of a muddy hue;
'Tis entrammeled in a mysterious web,
    Which Oceanus couldn't escape through.

The sea is just ahead
    Into which it silently pours,
Not a ripple doth it shed
    On bidding farewell its shores.

Similar is the picture of the pen,
    Portrayed by the bards divine,
Human Life begins and ends
    The same as this river of mine.

I have been thinking in the meanwhile
    Of a more simple plan:
Why not represent it with a crocodile
    Pursuing a frightened African?

When the darkey from danger was free,
    The crocodile being fast asleep,
Let this correspond to infancy,
    When at its own wants it weeps.

When the darkey first sights his pursuer
    From a safe distance in the wood,
Of no danger he is sure—
    This is coeval to thoughtless childhood.

The crocodile creeps on,
    The darkey hastens not aloof,
But remains steadfast and yawns—
    This is paramount to dauntless youth.

The crocodile advances with open jaws,
    Close to where its victim stood,
The darkey having fled, obeying safety's laws—
    This portrays vigorous manhood.

The darkey sinks deep in the mire
  Imprisoned in a fatal cage,
His devourer advances, full of ire—
  This corresponds to helpless old age.

The crocodile sweeps his destructive tail,
  And its fatal jaws together close,
The victim utters a single wail—
  His spirit to the hereafter goes.

MY FIRST ACQUAINTANCE WITH THE "MERRY NINE."

When my youth was yet at dawn,
Methought myself transported to Helicon ;
In the graves I beheld gods divine,
And made acquaintance with the " Merry Nine."

Apollo gave unto me a lyre,
Attuned to melodies Æolian fair ;
But with my untaught hand
No symphony could I command.

There were no mortals to jeer and hiss,
Because my harp played amiss ;
The benign muses, one and all,
My uncouth song extolled.

With their hands delicate, white,
With sparkling eyes like the stars of night,
With smiles heaven-engendered,
Made sweetest music I ever heard.

When their ovation was through,
They tuned my disconsonant harp anew ;
And when my fingers went astray
They taught them symphony.

O that I could have tarried here
Till the close of my earthly career!
Then this cold deceptionable world,
Its austere gonfanon would ne'er have unfurled.

To this prosaic life I were doomed to return,
And my poetic taper dimly burned,
To be shammed and snuffed,
By life's environments vigorously rough.

To feel, to partake of cold apathy,
That hang like apples of Sodom from each
    tree,
To endure contention—strife, though unsought,
Has been, as it ever must be, my lot.

There's little left to surprise,
There's nothing to betear my eyes,
Joy long ago was overthrown,
Melancholy and I stalk the world alone.

I have donned the Stoic's stole,
Hope, fear, joy, sorrow, move not my soul,
This drear life to me doth prove,
There's nothing to despise, little to love.

MY BARNS I WILL PULL DOWN

My barns I will pull down,
    Build them anew on larger foundation;
A bounteous harvest doth abound,
    I prosper in my vocation.

Heavier grows that iron-bound chest,
    Containing goodly treasures;
Mammon hath me blest,
    I'll give o'er to pleasure.

Hay I made while the sun shone,
   And the loft is ready to burst ;
Cattle on a thousand hills I own,
   What more can I thirst ?

I yearn for the coy glance
   Of maidens, handsome, **gay,**
For the mazy dance,
   And sparkling wine for **aye.**

O give me jolly comrades
   Whose nocturnal hours are **mellow,**
Jubilant while others are sad—
   A whole-souled lot of fellows.

Give me moonlit strolls in the **park,**
   With a fair lady companion,
From whose sparkling eye dark,
   Merriment in rills doth run.

Give me music, voluptuously **sweet,**
   And admittance to the ball-room ;
Give me Mercury's winged feet,
   That I may glide o'er the gloom.

I long to see the wide, wide world,
   To travel through foreign lands ;
To hear the buffoon and shun the churl,
   In fact all that Pleasure commands.

Hark, somebody is calling without
   The voice is not familiar ;
Surely there's no danger about.
   Only the good come near.

On my door the stranger raps,
   And my fears are adawed ;
'Tis a lone wanderer perhaps,
   In the darkness bewildered, awed.

Again he raps, loudly knocks,
  From my couch I'll not arise;
" Hold ! the door is locked !"
  He continues rapping to my surprise.

" Just step round the other side,
  Where you'll find an open door,
When within with me abide,
  Till darkness is o'er."

To my displeasure he still raps on
  Disregarding my kind invitation ;
" Ho, there ! disturbing the peace will be the
    caption
  That will enthrall you in the station."

" Thou fool this very night—"
  " Thou audacious intruder," I interpose,
" Pray what may be your right
  Such assertions to disclose ? "

" My authority is through the tomb,
  I am Death, on a mission bent ;
On thee I pass thy doom,
  E'er dawn thou shalt die ! be content."

In worldly Pleasure I put my trust.
  My way to happiness she paved,
O Christ, thou art unjust,
  Calling me to the loathsome grave !

On my brow gathers the death-damp,
  Fierce pains through my frame fly,
Dim grows my brilliant lamp,
  O God ! I swoon, I die.

A UTOPIAN DREAM.

Down beside Los Angeles sparkling stream,
    Where soft winds through orange blossoms stole,
I laid myself to rest, and dreamed,
    That bright youth again o'er me rolled.

The drear heavy years that clog the soul,
    Wasting the mind—stiffening the supple limb,
Wert, as in those good days of old,
    Sealed in Pandora's box within a cavern dim.

Then came one in angel-form, mortal is she,
    And laid soft hands upon my aching brow,
My heavy heart again beat free,
    As it will never more, I trow.

O'er her face there stole a smile
    Which my unschooled pen fails to portray.
'Twas something akin to that of a child's
    When children are met on a holiday.

Her bright dark eyes met mine: of woe
    In them methought there were a tear.
If such there was it did glow
    Like stars when the firmament is cold and clear.

She spoke. So musical were her tones,
    That I cast a glance up to the skies.
'Twas needless— they were her own,
    Blended with divine harmonies.

The years since I have beheld her form
    Shrunk to nothingness—closed like a scroll,
Or the morning-glory at past-morn,
    Or as wither flowers when winds blow cold.

The verdant orange bough waved o'er head,
    Pendent clung the golden fruit,
Here our vows anew we plighted,
    And strung to connubial bliss our lute.

Wavelets on the stream glistened,
  The odorous wind partook of our joy,
Birds sang blithe, they had listened
  To what death alone could destroy.

I clasped her hand—forth we strolled
  'Neath skies uncommonly serene,
Never was there a story told
  Of fairer skies of such celestial-descended scenes.

She grew pensively silent, to her I spoke.
  Lo ! she vanished in empty air,
The enchanted spell was broke,
  Leaving me to plod on in despair.

MISANTHROPY.

The chimeric esteem of friends is gone,
  And my youth is fast going.
  Like a monsoon o'er fertile lands blowing,
Withering all in its course, the morn
Of my life passed by. In the balances of Distrust,
Is weighed my existence—just or unjust.

As I assert, the fantastic illusion of friends
  And their friendship is gone. It doesn't matter
    much,
  'Twas like the using of a cane or crutch,
When each limb in obedience did attend
The bidding of my will. The friend we esteem to-day
May on the morrow become a nefarious enemy.

True friendship is like looking for teeth in the mouth
  Of the Father of Waters, full-bloomed sun-flowers
    in May,
  Cucumbers in December, in March new-mown hay,
Thunder, lightning and rain during protracted
    drought,
Christmas or New Years to occur in June,
Or moon-lit nights in the dark of the moon.

THE DISTANT FUTURE.

In the distant future an alien race will flourish
   On our plains, o'er our tombs, 'mid our ruins. Our
      philosophy
   Will be so elevated that 'tis now in its infancy,
Some strange creed will gratify the wish
Of him who desires to worship. And, in short,
Our religion will be wholly forgot.

When these aliens have outlived their day—
   Which may be much longer than ours—
   They will succumb to Nature's powers.
Throughout their domains desolation will prey
Upon their possessions. Large cities habitantless,
'Mid unbroken silence will crumble to nothingness.

On and on revolves the earth, all tenantless,
   The gigantic forest is leveled to the ground,
   The torrent in the mount ceases to sound.
All is enshrouded in Stygian darkness.
Out upon the sullen sea icebergs thunder
As they collide and part asunder.

The earth has become infirm with years—
   Like man she was born, like man
   She must die. When nearing the strand
She may collide with a planet that careers
From its orbit. With awful crash
All will end like lightning's flash.

A TEMPEST.

In the west distant thunder rolls,
   The solid hills seem to tremble. The foliage
   Hangs motionless. Not a zephyr breathes on the
      page
Of quietude. Nature with difficulty controls
Her composure. Impenetrable is the gloom—
A tempest its vehement mood is to assume,

Gloom o'ercasts the land entire,
  Broken at intervals by heavy thunder.
  The waters of lake and river quake with wonder.
Birds have sought their safety.   The lurid fire
Here and there descends in the forest;
Many a noble tree is laid to waste.

After brief interval, on comes the tempest,
  Accompanied by wind of great strength:
  Trees are uprooted and lie at full length,
Rocks shake in their ancient nest,
Torrents gush everywhere, down the vale they pour,
Striving Niagara Falls to outroar.

JUVENILE ASPIRATIONS.

From this monotonous farm life I yearn to be far
    away,
  Here transpires nothing more than takes place
  In the hackneyed walks of life, marring the face
Of my romantic idol with monotony;
I yearn to blow bubbles of excitement and strife
From the pipe unsmoked in every-day life.

Soon may I depart for the wild west,
  To hunt bison and bear, to trap beaver.
  Adroitly as the butcher with his cleaver,
With my bowie-knife I would lay the Indian at rest;
I would draw ichor through the hero's straw
On wooing my vanquished antagonist's squaw.

On a bronco I would ride as a whirlwind
  Over interminable plains; with my lariat
  Every refactory critter I would upset;
I would spin yarns; those who did them rescind
Why, sir, I would draw my gun,
And laugh at the tragedy as if it were fun.

A BAD BOY.

A bad boy in the gloam
    Toward a deacon's orchard took his way.
On perceiving the owner was not at home
    Leaped the fence with spirits gay,
And began putting forbidden fruit,
Into pockets that always did apples suit.

When pockets were full a suspender he tied around
    The bottom of his coat sleeve—making a small bag.
When filled, it was quite heavy, but found,
    'Neath such a burden he would not fag,
Yet he did not intend to go so far
As to burden himself like a pack-peddler.

The other sleeve was filled full as the first,
    Thus the burden being doubled, and yet more
He could carry. The lining of his vest he burst
    And stowed away as many as before.
He beheld a sight, on stooping to take up the burden,
That made a frightful thrill through his soul run.

The swiftest pace a canine can fly on,
    With tongue a-lolling, came a monstrous Newfound-
        land.
He leveled his derringer and fired. Poor Lion
    Yelled, leaped high, dropped lifeless in the sand.
On not quite so swift a run
Came the deacon, bearing a shot-gun.

" Ho, there ! " cried the bad boy, with derringer ready
    for action,
    Stop ! or I will drop you in your tracks ;
See," pointing out the carcass, "to kill is a faction
    Of my earthly calling. What devilment it lacks
I will call on you to fill the void,
As with Satan's dross you're alloyed.

" My stars ! whose boy are you ? "
   Inquired the astonished deacon.
'Tis the old tempter that imbues
   Our motley eyes to gaze on such a beacon.
I declare, my young borrower of Peter to pay Paul,
That this night in prison you shall fall ! "

" Ah, ah, old gent, take a drink,"
   Said the young scapegrace, extending a flask :
" My situation is not so dreadful as you think.
   I try to give satisfaction, what more can you ask ?
As you will not indulge in a friendly cup,
Say we play a game at seven-up."

" My sakes ! whose boy can you be ? "
   Asked the deacon advancing a step or two ;
The presented pistol did not quite agree
   With his ideas of safety. Presently, in lieu
Of farther questioning, he grew bolder,
Intending to lay a heavy hand on the lad's shoulder.

He was smitten with a pair of brass-knuckles
   Square in the face. The blow broke his nose ;
With a mysterious groan, a sort of chuckle,
   Which bespoke him in extreme throes,
He turned a complete somersault
As if in acrobatic art taught.

Full-length upon the ground he lay,
   Rigid as the canine's lifeless carcass.
The victor, who by the way
   Had not received a scratch in the fracas,
Stood triumphant o'er his antagonist like David
With sword aloft to strike off Goliath's head.

" Think I had better go after the old man,
   I am sure he is badly hurt,"
Mused the bad boy (the sand
   In the deacon's life's hourglass being still inert).

Few paces he had strode on his way
When the deacon was heard to pray.

He returned, and beside his booty sat,
   Listening to the deacon's devotions:
"Pshaw! we will pass around the hat,
   You need not relate your strange notions.
'Tis out of season for boys to be pious;
Think it not true? why, sir, just try us."

His own hat was held close in his face
   The same as he presented it to the congregation;
When each deemed it out of place
   To give unto the Lord. Their avocation
Was giving unto Satan instead,
In which not one was close-fisted.

"I recognize you now," the deacon moaned
   Peering through his own gore;
"I pray that round your neck a millstone
   May be tied, and a thousand miles from shore
Be cast overboard, head-foremost,
That a shark devour even your ghost."

MISTY TRADITION.

'Tis through tradition that unto us is given
The mysteries of our origin—of all things;
From beginning to end with uncertainty 'tis riven.
Collusive as the argument the Sophist brings,
Ever since the scribe began to wield the pen,
Much collusive tradition there has been.

In tradition 'tis not essential to take much stock.
It avers the Pilgrims landed on Forefathers' Rock;
Of William Tell it categorically declares
He shot an apple from the head of his heir;
No one will doubt, if such the facts were,
That he was the champion archer.

Father Washington, from whom King George III.
Strove for years, with cannon and sword,
To snatch our Independence, though he failed to
    snatch it;
Cut his father's favorite cherry-tree with his little
    hatchet,
We know not whether this injury caused the tree to
    die,
"Father, I did it," he exclaimed, "I cannot tell a
    lie."

Another remarkable event Tradition doth amass,
The rescue of Captain John Smith by Pocahontas.
He who wishes can consider it the truth.
Also that Ponce de Leon discovered the Fountain of
    Youth
Among the drear morasses of Florida,
Where fever and pestilence tarry alway.

THE THREE EVENTS.

There are three events in life that usually
    Attract attention : First, our birth; second, our
      wedding—
That is should we see fit to obey
    The will of Cupid; third, our death. Each event
      brings
Forth our best clothes somewhere to go,
A merry-making or to let mournful tears flow.

At the first event there's joy,
    At the second the same till wanes the honeymoon,—
This evanescent orb two weeks doth destroy,—
    The third event, the flitiferous doom
Of him, rigid in everlasting sleep,
Brings forth saddest tears,—mortal weeps.

THE BELLS.

Sweet is the jingle of sleigh bells,
  That on a moonlit winter's eve wrinkle,
  The air with music jingling to the twinkle
Of the stars. From the wedding bell
Sweet are the peals. But unwelcome is the sound
That calls the school-boy in from the play-ground.

High in heaven's great belfry
  Are hung a set of chimes,
  Sweeter, clearer, than Pindaric rhymes;
Each morn heaven's diapason plays
As Aurora opes her golden gates,
And Sol appears in his august state.

Sweet bell in the belfry old,
  With claritude swelling on the evening air,
  Calling us together for prayer,
What messages of goodwill you've told!
And at the hour of midnight drear,
Ringing a requiem to the old year.

FOURTH OF JULY.

A day of glory is the Fourth of July.
  Conspicuous are the stars and stripes,
  The eagle soaring at a lofty height,
Looks down, and seems to cry.
"O Liberty! take wing, with me soar
Over the 'land of the free' evermore."

O let the brazen cannon roar,
  Let the boy explode his fire-crackers,
  Let the orator with Bacchus
Quaff of ice-cold nectar;
'Tis a day to remembered be,
'Tis the day of sweet Liberty.

1·

Let the brass bands play the airs
   Of " America," " Hail Columbia,"
   " The Star-Spangled Banner," so free
Waves from everywhere.
Wave ! wave ! O stripes and stars,
The sons of freedom we are.

WINONA.

Since " truth is stranger than fiction,"
   I lay aside all fictious whims and settle
   Down on truth, solid truth, whose mettle
Is never tinctured with doubt.   Within restriction
Of the bard I may with awkward stride,
Place Truth and Doubt side by side.

A true story I am about to commence,
   A story that will in the minds of all
   Kindle the love of the truth, and, if called
Upon by you, reader, to vindicate an offence
Common to authors—that of being stupid—
Remember, this story has but recently entered my
     head.

A true story I have promised, you say,
According to tradition it occurred near Winona,
     Minnesota.
Where the Father of Waters yet continues to smile
On primeval forests, on bluffs abrupt and wild,
And particularly on one huge rock towering above
     the rest,
Which seems anxious to plunge into the river's
     breast.

'Twas here where dwelt the noble Sioux,
Who lifted scalps at Red Wing and Earth Blue,
Early in the sixties.   Here they no longer range,
Save the forest bluffs and river all is changed ;

Where used to be their hunting-ground
Habitations of the whites thickly abound.

Winona, the heroine, was of uncommon loveliness,
Being with every charm of maidenhood blest.
Over her beauty a civilized belle would have gone wild;
In fact, she was nature's favored child.
Unfortunately, she was possessed of an alien lover,
Whom her sire with disapprobation covered.

I know not, as it matters little, the name of my hero,
A young hunter of the Wapashas. He was not at
    all below
The standard of his numerous fellow-warriors:
On several occasions, by the light of the stars,
Had vanquished his enemy, killed his bear,
And the sun-dance he performed with valor.

I regret to say that between this loving pair
There was, as invariably the case is, an impassable
    barrier.
Her sire—as grim a warrior as ever threw a toma-
    hawk,
Shot an arrow, raised a scalp, or chew the cork
From his white friend's bottle—was not in favor
With the doings of these steadfast lovers.

He, like many a sire in Christian lands,
Had selected for her heart and hand
A distinguished personage—a young brave, who saw
His glory spring from slaying the hostile Chippewas,
Whom he slew with ease in many a gory affray
Like grass that's mown down for hay.

She cared not to share his fadeless laurels,
Won through bloodshed, but deemed it nobler to
    quarrel
With her parents concerning her future welfare,—
Quarrels on such a subject will, as I aver,

Always bring an adequate, even exorbitant, price,
So long as Cupid does the young to parental conten-
    tion entice.

This was the sole instance he ever frowned
Upon his only child. She yearned for the dawn
Of a tranquil season. With eloquence she related
    her tale.
He listened attentively. Her entreaties were of no
    avail.
Half-involuntarily I pen : how out of reason,
Are all civilized or uncivilized Pa's on such occasion.

In the glen of doubt the young hunter could no
    longer grope,
So he, like a civilized lover, planned to elope.
He chose the dark of the moon or a cloudy night,
When storm-clouds through heaven would take
    flight,—
Then he could in security steal his prize away
Like one after having committed owlry.

Many times he rehearsed his preparations,
Such as stealing cautiously by from his station,
Darting here and there behind a tree, or through
Tangled wood to where his canoe,
The best among the fleet, was tied.
As a paddler, of his race he was the pride.

He was, as we see, a determined lover,
Such as is found within the wood's covers,
But in real life rather exotic. How uncool
Were we in youth while waiting in the vestibule
After church for our fair ones to come out!
Often did fear of rejection put our good intentions
    to route.

On a certain night, the door he approached and it
    unloosed.
A startled cry from an adopted papoose

Awoke all within. The grim old sire,
Grasped his war-club, into darkness sprung full of ire
On his flight, vengeance again and again he swore,
On him who broke his tranquil slumber.

The watch-dog scented the intruder's trail,
Which led through a thicket and down a vale,
Which a short distance from the river ends in a gulf.
Presently the old warrior re-entered his lodge and
      exclaiming, " Ugh, a wolf.
Soon as morning dawns, and the mists clear away,
A severe forfeit the prowling beast shall pay."

On a soft couch of deer and bear skins lay **Winona**,
Apparently asleep, though she could gainsay
The real intruder. Her sighs and sobs were stifled,
But now and then a moan escaped—she was baffled,
And how keen must have been the disappointment.
To those thus afflicted, a tear or two I give vent.

He came again on a cloudy night ; the moon was full,
And a dense fog all at once began to pull
Its misty mantle close around the landscape ;
Dripped every twig; wet to the skin was he ; with
      the cape,
Of unquieted love about his shoulders, and, with his
      zealous endeavor,
Cared little for condition of the weather.

'Twas at the tranquil hour of midnight, when cau-
      tiously
This ardent lover groped his way
'Mong various lodges to his sweetheart's wigwam,
Pitched 'neath a maple shattered by storms.
He was elated more than words can tell
On finding the watch-dog asleep in its world-wide
      kennel.

He arrived not with a close carriage
To bear her away; no license of marriage
Had he.   No servants were bribed to procure a ladder
And place it 'gainst her chamber window—still sadder,
The watch-dog had not been poisoned or shot.
Dogs generally are quick at discovering such a plot.

He gazed long and wistfully at her lodge,
Turned back, concluding it was best to dodge
The hazardous undertaking.   Presently his courage
     returned,
Within his whole frame the fire of determination
     burned,
Making him bold, nerving him to such a state,
That he cared little what might be his fate.

However, he was betrayed by a snorting pony in the
     yard grazing
Lo! at the lodge door stood the old warrior, star-
     gazing,
Who gazed at a single star that had appeared
In the west, when sky and bluffs each other neared.
While gazing on this orb evanescently brief,
His loved one, Winona, gave way to grief.

Many interrogatories concerning her grief were pro-
     pounded
By her sire, who at length became confounded
At her silence—painful to him as that which takes
     place
When death steals o'er his last enemy's face,
Or the last glow from a consumed village,
Which his band without resistance pillaged.

Winona's mother, as obedient a matron
As ever prepared her lord's meal, or hoed a hill of
     corn,
Came to her bedside and whispered in her ear,
Receiving in reply few pantomimic gestures, as if
     fear

Had control of her speech. She pointed to the
     spring
That at the foot of the hill was silently gushing.

They, that is, Winona and her mamma,
Put on their head-gear and went forth. The same
     star,
And two or three more, shone through
A rent in the clouds. The moon, askew
In a large rent, made her unwelcome appearance
That is, to Winona, who teemed with innocence.

Their mission was not uncommon, nothing daring
About it. Her mother had often taken her out for
     an airing
At all hours of day or night. In my opinion no
     blame
Can be heaped upon the indulgent mother. A civ-
     ilized mamma does the same ;
In rich attire she and her daughter pace the street
     to and fro,
Hoping to win the heart and hand of a wealthy beau.

They passed on, their tongues keeping up a clatter ;
They talked of the fields of maize, that at the latter
Part of October would be ready to gather in,
Of near relations that for years had been
In the happy hunting-ground. They mentioned the
     foe,
But were silent on their deeds of woe.

The foliage rustled, their confab ceased.
The matron feared that in ambush crouched a wild
     beast,
Awaiting them to draw near. Above her—
Rather above them both—was Winona's lover,
On a rainbow like tree-trunk in attitude of a puma,
To spring down on his intended mother-in-law.

The spring was reached without further interruption.
Winona stood, Rebecca-like, amd gave her mother one
Long, deep quaff from a small birchen vessel.
As she dipped it the second time a dreadful yell
And cries for help escaped the lips of her poor mam-
        ma,
As if she were overpowered by a panther.

Winona at the same moment shrieked,
And sank upon the ground.   In this attitude a voice
        did speak
To her as follows: "Winona, be not afraid, 'tis I,
Your lover; for the river make haste, O fly!
To escape, this is our only chance.
For the river by our secret path, advance."

She recovered, and waited not a second invitation.
On glancing over her shoulder—I think the left one—
She saw an unique struggle between her mother and
      ' lover,
His clothes were rent in shreds, and all over
His manly face—save where it was gored—
Mere artistic finger-marks like the squares of a
        checker-board.

In the mutable moonlight the scuffle was dire,
The villagers came forth, headed by the sire,
Who, for the first time since childhood, had left his
        bow behind,—
'Tis strange that many others were equally as blind;
The fact is the only one to negligence remained neu-
        ter
Was the young warrior—Winona's rejected suitor.

Without shaking hands, the young hunter left the
        old lady,
And fled through the thicket.   Howling as rejoices a
        May-day

Party of children, both great and small circling round
     the pole,
Departed the avengers, fully armed. Their keen
     cold
Weapons gleamed in the lambent moonbeams,
Which now descended in broad silvery streams.

" For the villain's capture, I will give ten ponies,"
Vociferated the ill-treated matron in tones sardonic—
     stony,
And my Winona, my own Winona, O, where
Has she fled? " She wrung her hands and tore her
     hair,
" Great Spirit, on the villain, I call down thy wrath,
As the avenger, may thou too, go on the warpath."

She crept back to the deserted wigwam.
Her indignation burst forth in one grand storm ;
The vituperation none could withstand.
To quiet her with his talismanic art, came the medi-
     cine man,
And the uproar they both created
Resembled that in Congress when Mill's Bill was de-
     bated.

Every male joined in the exciting chase,
The dotardic grandsire, with drawn bow, with slow
     pace,
Plodded on. Young braves bounded like deers
Through the forest—excitement grew intense—fear,
Their long-absent comrade, returned not to imbue
Them with cowardice as on they flew.

Now over a fallen tree or mossy stone
Many fell, augmenting the clamorous tone.
The trail of the fleeing couple grew less distinct ;
And presently it was lost on the bluff's brink.
Some advocated they had plunged o'er the abyss,
While others, that the right course was missed.

Far down 'mong the shrubs and stones
Many imagined they heard groans ;
Prostrate on the brink, with hands above his eyes,
Gazed the worthy sire.   Fear nor surprise,
If at all in his mind dwelt, changed not his visage,
Among the Stoics he was a sage.

He gazed protracted with an exile-like gaze,
Who looks on his native land when distance begins
        to haze
It from his sight.   In similar postures
Were many more.   The majority were sure
The elopers had unintentionally ended themselves ;
That their mangled remains were on two small
        shelves.

In rising, the sire lost his equilibrium,
And disappeared in the depths below.   All dumb
With surprise, if not with horror, stood his comrades.
Soon as they could speak some pronounced it acci-
        dental, others a mad
Attempt at self-destruction, such as consider life
        vanity,
Whom the public pronounce, subjects of temporary
        insanity.

After brief interval came groans in reality,
A torch was lowered ; in the fork of a tree,
Not fork really, but between two large splinters,
Absalom-like, by the hair hung the old warrior,
Dangling to and fro. His eagle feather head-dress
Had lodged in a shrub not far from the crest.

The question arose: How were they to effect a
        rescue ?
At length out spoke the wisest of the crew ;
" Through his obstinacy Winona's and young hun-
        ter's lives are ended,
Here by the hair let him remain suspended
As hangs the bad white man by the neck,
Till vultures his bones have picked."

" We must save him," the rejected suitor demurred,
" Your suggestions, like yourself, are absurd ;
Of all sires he is the most indulgent,
I cannot understand what Winona meant
By eloping with that bear-killing swain,
Who an able enemy has never slain."

The suitor they heeded ; one began scaling the bluff.
He did well, as the descent was rough.
When nearing the sire, or old warrior, lost his foot-
      hold,
And with a headlong plunge, seemingly bold,
He struck the water with heavy splash,
Lifeless, as if to fragments dashed.

There were none to mourn his untimely end,
Nor to look sad would one condescend.
Each and all were of inflexible mold,
Such as becomes the Stoic in his stole.
These children of nature, barbarians rude,
With olden time stoicism were imbued.

Cautiously down the bluff another one crept,
His eyes on safety close he kept ;
With the aid of a bough, sapling, or grape vine,
He lowered himself. And each time
That an obstacle thwarted his descent,
Without difficulty over it he went.

At the foot of the tree he now stood,
And found the old warrior in painful mood,
Suspended from the ground high as the top of the
      sour apple tree,
On which Jeff. Davis' soul was to be set free ;
But this great votary of the "fallen cause "
Was destined to live on till Nature set her pause.

A mode of rescue had now come over the old warrior's
      mind :
He placed a hand against each splinter, and did find

An upward way, at which he labored well;
With desperate struggle loosened his hair and fell
To the ground, landing upon his feet with ease,
And from exhaustion smote together his knees.

He stood in silence, not a murmur was heard,
On his countenance there rested a bewildered
And fatigued expression.   After brief interval
He began ascending the bluff, almost inaccessible.
When ascending to where his weapons lay,
He paused few moments and resumed his upward
    way.

Different it was with the young brave, who found,
After many attempts, he could neither get up nor go
    down,
There was but one recourse—which he chose
Rather than remain here and endure throes
Of thirst and hunger—with a wild leap
He disappeared forever in waters deep.

" They have made good their escape," the old warrior
    exclaimed to those around him,
" The Great Spirit is grieved that we have not found
    him.
Behold, my children," pointing to the sullen waters,
" In peace I could die if there reposed my daughter,
But to know she has wed that servile fox,
Shall within a single moon whiten these raven
    locks."

Quoth the rejected suitor, " my father, do not despair,
I have thrice in darkness tracked bruin to his lair,
By starlight followed the enemy's concealed trail.
Ere yon moon in the light of day pales
I swear you shall behold him a captive bound,
And beloved Winona at your lodge will be found.

Continued the rejected suitor: " Am sure, indulgent
    father,
They have ere this time crossed the river, or, rather,

Through fear of being overtaken, they fled to that
    island
Which lies almost within an arrow's flight of this high-
    land.
There the sycamore and ash tower in grace,
For the romantic, such as they are, is just the place."

After thus speaking he began examining the ground.
To his delight the elopers' footprints were found.
Instead of going over the brink they turned to the
    left,
Following along the crest till coming to a cleft.
Which, reader, you will remember, was "the secret
    path "
The young hunter spoke of when Winona and her
    mother from the spring quaffed

This was a natural thoroughfare through the ledge,
Leading within few yards of the water's edge ;
Here a rock that had fallen from above its jagged
    form uplifted,
Against it one of their canoes had drifted.
They were not aware of a hole in the stern, it being
    dark.
In the canoe beside the old warrior and suitor, six of
    them embarked.

They pushed out, and with the aid of two paddles,
That had lodged with her they shot forward. All
    seemed addled.
Not one noticed the water pouring through the rent.
With their hands for paddles speed they did aug-
    ment,
To the island bound, and when midway,
Without warning the craft bottom up did lay.

There was confusion 'mong the grim crew.
With affection-like embrace four of them threw
Arms around each other's necks, and sank to rise no
    more.
The old warrior was afloat on an oar.

The rejected suitor had mounted the inverted canoe,
And called loudly for aid in his rescue.

Apart these survivors are drifting,
Each trying to reach shore. Scarcely lifting
His head above the surface is the old warrior. He
    shouts,
But the water pouring down his throat routs
His sonorous tones. In his ears there's a hum.
He attempts to shout but finds himself dumb.

What! must he perish thus? Ah, no!
A single canoe containing two occupants row
To his aid. With difficulty he is rescued,
On his benefactors, gratitude he strews,
The voice is familiar. "Great Spirit, horrors!
'Tis father, who will alarm all the warriors."

Thus spoke a maid—no other than Winona, who,
With her lover, was making an escape to
The other side. "You old wretch with this oar,"
Spoke the young hunter, "I shall end you before
You make known our whereabouts. I will bring it
    down
Sending you to the happy hunting-ground."

"Strike not! Grant my life is all I ask,
And henceforth you shall not be tasked
With my ingratitude. Let strife cease;
When ashore we will smoke the pipe of peace.
You have proven yourself worthy of my beloved
    child
Though sought by another on whom distinction
    smiles.

"Can I rely upon what you say?
If you will swear by the moon taking her way
Through the heavens, I will take you ashore.
Should you prove false your life is good as o'er.
Who among us is so base as the liar?
More to be dreaded than the annual prairie fire."

With uplifted hand the old warrior took an oath in
      accents faint,
As s'wore the ancients o'er the bones of Christian
      saints;
But had no intention of keeping his oath.
He longed for his blood and to break Winona's
      troth.
Noble Red Man he may be designated,
But never was there a greater villain created.

While arranging some unimportant affairs,
Canoes came around them in pairs ;
No arms were visible—on the craft's bottom they were
      stowed
And from each face treachery glowed
Winona glanced disdainfully in the face of her rival,
Which told him his ardent regards were trivial.

In silence they proceeded up stream,
Each ripple bore a phosphorescent gleam
At this early hour—half-past three o'clock.
A crow was heard from the prairie cock,
From the orient the first effulgence of morn
O'er the broad river quiet was borne.

They arrived at an inlet, their canoes were moored,
The young hunter now became aware by falsehood
      he was allured.
Yet, not a symptom of fear did he betray ;
Both he and Winona grew hilariously gay.
They were looked upon as do we the silly moth
That flits round our lamp till burning its wings off.

With malignant smiles the rejected suitor advanced,
(On him Winona cast the same disdainful glance)
" Ah, Ah," he chuckled, " my killer of muskrats ;
You little know what you've been at.
'Tis for my Winona's and your own good sake
That at noonday we burn you at the stake."

"What means this?" the young hunter demanded of
   Winona's sire,
"By all that's holy did you not swear
That we should be steadfast friends,
Till the Great Spirit for us sends?
You wolf!" addressing the suitor all in smiles,
"The Chippewas possess not half your wiles."

To Winona her father spoke thus:
"My child, to wed this fox I trust
Is not your intention. At once give him the mitten;
That is, drop him, as a pale face drops a bag of
   kittens.
Accept the favors of him whose chief-like craft
In the face of every danger laughs."

She placed her arms about his neck,
And sobbed "How can I? For your choice I have
   no respect;
Without whom I love how can life be borne?
Leave me here alone. Let me mourn
Till the Great Spirit arrives, in whose arms
I can rest secure from every harm."

She spoke the true sentiments of her heart.
The rejected suitor, who at the start
So presumptuous, was appalled now;
He staggered as if receiving a death-blow.
And threw himself at her feet prostrate.
A civilized lover sometimes assumes this inept state.

"My child," continued the sire, "I have but one word
   to say:
Comply with my request or take the penalty.
Till yon cloud obscures the moon you have to make
Up your mind. Winona, listen, for my sake.
Will you obey? On every hand in ambush
Lie warriors, who will do whatever I wish."

"Let them come," responded the gallant lover.
He examined his trusty bow and from his quiver
Drew an arrow of extra-finish.   With this arrow
I compelled the high-soaring eagle to throw
Aside his lofty flight.   And with this tomahawk
I have silenced many an enemy's talk."

The cloud obscured the moon.   Shouted the sire,
    " Take them ! "
On came a dozen warriors, like a pack of hounds
    chasing a fox to den.
At the foremost, his rival, he took deliberate aim
And laid him prostrate.   A young brave he lamed,
This wounded brave, with good intention,
Limped to the chief's lodge to make applications for a
    pension.

At him came arrows in every conceivable shape,
From being wounded he miraculously escaped;
At length an arrow penetrated his thigh
Which made him furious—uttering his war-cry.
He sprang forth, as leaps the kangaroo,
And with tomahawk an enemy slew.

Winona, of extraordinary pluck,
Hid behind a tree and cried at the ill-luck;
Of being harmed she had little fear,
As her weapons of defence were tears.
Tears she shed in profusion;
Not one of them were of collusion.

The young hunter retreated behind the same tree,
And fought like a hero of Thermopylae.
His presence nerved Winona, who grasped a fallen
    brave's bow
Which proved more destructive than her hero's.
Think you, reader, woman cannot fight ? Try her on.
What said those redcoats in facing Molly Stark's flat-
    irons ?

12

More numerous flew the keen-pointed missiles,
Some with heavy thud penetrated far in the tree,
    but still
They did no harm.—Demanded the sire, " You rebel,
    surrender ! "
" I will fight it out on this line, if it takes all sum-
    mer ! "
Responded the hero. From help of putting this asser-
    tion in his mouth I can't,
For it is the very words of immortal Grant.

They were flanked, fighting at fearful odds.
" Winona, make haste for the rocks, or the gods
Will see us perish here." Towards the rocks she flew.
He began retreating, and put daylight through
Half a dozen of his pursuers, who were amazed
At the rapid manner they were razed.

The rock, an isolated one, is a natural tower.
On reviewing it one almost believes that the Supreme
    Power,
After having fashioned the precipitous bluffs,
Deposited this fragment here as material enough
He already had. Thus it stands in grandeur sable,
Wanting a top as did the Tower of Babel.

At the base it is a hundred yards around ; eighty feet
    in height.
And stands at the mouth of a miniature bight,
Once their harbor. Difficult is the ascent ;
In the back are hewn few shallow steps, not twenty
    in extent,
Is the only means of reaching the summit ;
The difficulty is great, few care to overcome it.

She reached the rock, when she had ascended,
Her lover stood at the base, whom she defended
By casting down on the enemy stones.
One struck her sire and fractured a thigh bone,

Another fell upon the head of a young brave,
Of course it prepared him for the grave.

When within a step or two of the crest,
The young hunter received an arrow in the chest.
He would have fallen to the ground save Winona,
Who grasped his hand and drew him out of harm's
    way.
There was something in his face
Telling her that soon would close his race.

Upon the crest of this rock there stood a single cedar
With its long serpentine roots, clinging tenaciously,
    as if it were
Afraid of losing its shallow footing; its gnarly
    trunk
Was nothing more than a huge bundle of splinters—
    shrunk
From many limbs was the bark. And with glad
    surprise
It caught the first gleam of sunrise.

The lovers sought rest beneath its half-dead branches,
And looked down at the warriors squatted on their
    haunches,
Like some beast of prey watching its victim.
Not a savage spoke till the sire who could stem
Silence no longer said, " Winona, if you will come
    down,
You and your lover 'mong us friends will have found."

" Father," replied she, "in keeping your promise you
    deceived me.
You have offended the Great Spirit, which grieves me.
From your treachery we are safe up here ;
If at sunset no other way of escape appears,
In the river we will end our career—
My lover is dying ; Great Spirit, draw near ! "

The sky at the east was now luminous,
Her sable bands night was about to burst,
A belt of golden radiance extended from horizon
To zenith. Morn in her beauty was jocund,
And never did there on this land dawn,
A more beautiful yet flitiferous morn.

In the water near the surface, swam fishes,
Goodly in size, of bright colors fit for dishes
Of presidents. And where shallow water flows,
Teemed with manifold species of minnows.
Some 'neath a stone sought to hide away
From large members of the finny tribe searching
    for prey.

In the bight swam geese and goslings,
The black swan floated unmolested, the white swan
    of dazzling
Whiteness mundified its plumage in the cool depths;
Frogs croaked, crickets chirped on the bank that steps
Off abruptly. In the damp grass the glow worm
    shone,
The skylark sang blithe from the celestial dome.

"Winona," whispered the dying lover, "it matters
    little now,
I am dying; my death will free you of your vows.
Return to your father, be an obedient child,
The Great Spirit and I will watch over you all the
    while.
When the full moon comes forth in her majestic pride
I will visit you, and we will walk side by side.

"Winona, my own Winona, farewell, farewell."
His cold, limp hand from hers fell.
"I will follow you, my gallant hero,"
Sobbed Winona, "I hate this life of woe!"
She advanced to the verge,
O'er which she plunged on singing her dirge.

THE DIRGE.

"Great Spirit, my sorrow forsooth,
  Soon I shall bury in the grave,
Slain is the love of my youth
  Whom to me joy ever gave.

" The deer finds refuge and peace
  In the depths of some sylvan glen.
Were I to flee there, like yeast
  Would froth the crime of these mad men.

" O dark, deep, ebbing river
  You can give me rest.
Of peace you are a giver,
  Receive me in your breast."

THE FATAL SHEARS.

Atropos has a pair of shears
  That clips life's brittle thread;
For above five thousand years,
  It has clipped for all the dead.

It clips at the dead of night,
  And all the hours within;
It ceases not in daylight,
  When Clotho and Lachesis spin.

A single clip and the king
  · Loses the Promethean fire;
It is a perpetual motion thing
  That never, never tires.

THE TRAVELLER'S RETURN.

Ripe hung the fruit on the apple tree,
  The grape vine was laden with abundance
The harvest field was blessed by Ceres,
  Of maize there was redundance.

Peace and plenty smiled o'er the land,
  Full to the brim was cornucopia;
Luxury had taken want by the hand,
  And led her far astray.

Squirrels, too, had gathered in
  Twofold their usual hoard;
Down rained brown nuts in the wind,
  Down like a shower they poured.

'Twas through this favored spot
  A traveller with youth yet aglow
Took his way unto a farm cot,
  And none did him know.

He gazed upon the familiar walls:
  With strange pictures they were hung;
Torn away was the little hall,
  Removed the door bell he oft had rung.

Departed, too, was the little fawn
  Who used to answer his ring;
Out in the world she had gone
  With her lord and king.

On a rustic seat he sought rest,
  And thought of other days,
Ere he a wanderer in the West
  Had learned life's austere ways.

He imagined she sat by his side,
   As in happy times gone by;
When the world was no more wide
   Than what's encompassed with the eye.

She told him of the weary hours
   For his return she had waited in vain,
Like upon the hills wild flowers
   Drooping for want of rain.

She mentioned the years that fleeted by,
   Of the vigil she kept,
And when hope began to die
   Of the many nights she wept.

" Woe unto me ! " he cried,
   And smote his breast with might;
" O, that I could have died
   Ere I beheld these familiar sights.

" Ah, " continued he with a groan,
   " Heaven's will be done !
I am but a rolling-stone
   That no moss can grow on.

" Let me return to my haunts,
   To some lone ocean cave ;
Few, very few, are my wants,
   My hopes are all in the grave.

" Is this what I have striven for ?
   The years of privation I underwent
Were but to open misfortune's door:
   God is good—my heart be content."

The traveller's hand stole to his face
   To brush away a single tear ;
He arose, left the place,
   Down the dusty road he disappeared.

' A SORCERESS.

There's a lovely picturesque woodland
Hard by the east shore of Lake Michigan,
On which the sun seems ever to shine.
In soft winds waves the tall pine,
And 'neath the wide spreading cedar
Prowls the wolf and bounds the deer.

The extent of this land is not great,
Much smaller than our Republic's smallest state ;
Near its centre a beautiful river rushes.
Just before emptying into the lake it gushes
O'er a small precipice, roaring loudly,
Thence in silence takes its way.

This river is beautiful, I know very well,
Its waters are cool, clear as crystal,
And 'tis said it flows o'er a bed of pearl
Similar to the river of the celestial world
That proceeds out the throne of God and the Lamb,
Beautifying heaven, so happy and calm.

Above the falls in a majestic bend
Is an island about the size of Island Number Ten
Through the centre proclivious hills rift,
Forming many a grotesque cave and cliff ;
And one huge rock I remember in particular,
Which has recently fallen into the river.

While this rock was in its ancient place,
The Indian built his camp-fire on its barren face
Or sat in stupid silence, when the sun was high,
Pondering heroic deeds long gone by,
Of when his sires and the brave paleface
With rifle and tomahawk strove to end each other's
      race.

In this most romantic spot of the West
There dwells, solitary, alone, a sorceress ;
And, strange as it may be,
She transforms men into beasts like Circe ;
On whom her magic she wrought last
Now possesses the form of an ass.

George Washington Jones Hawe was his name
While existing in a human frame ;
He was a mightier hunter than Nimrod,
And on a certain day overcame dreadful odds
In taking a young rodent—a muskrat—
From out the jaws of a polecat.

The wolf, bear and beaver he trapped,
Like Gideon's fearless warriors he lapped
From the brook when quenching his thirst,
Milo-like the skull of an ox he burst
With a single blow of the fist,
And snapped the head from off two critics that hissed.

When skies are warm and hills green, near a cavern,
Her summer residence, he grazes ;
And when autumn the sky hazes
He follows his mistress to her tavern
Or winter residence and through wintry days
He, like many a Midas-eared biped, incessantly brays.

In a corner of her summer residence a rosebush
    bloomed,
'Neath it were spread the skin of several deer,
Forming her couch.　Near it squatted her com-
    panion—queer
In being—a huge cinnamon bear that her art
    doomed,
To keep vigil whilst she reposed.
He kept at bay both friends and foes.

Bruin began pacing to and fro—each time
As he passed the couch whereon reclined his mis-
        tress
He touched his tongue to her cheek, or blest
Her with a hug quite superfine;
And we deemed it a grevious sin
That we were not Bruin.

Having with her partaken of a good meal,
She led us down an abrupt path
Through a narrow belt of wood, across a brook that
        laughs
On its way to the river, and thence into a wide field
Fenced with Gliden's patent barb wire
Which kept her pets from going below or coming
        higher.

She called,—side by side came a kid and panther;
They crouched at her feet and received her caresses,
A wolf and lamb came next.   A hyena that expresses
A human sort of grin tarried close by.   At her
Bidding it began laughing and skulked to the foliage
Wherein it paced to and fro as if it were caged,

From a fissure in a ledge came snakes
Of every variety and size.   The most venomous
Were harmless.   Around her arms they coiled; many
        did thrust
Out their forked tongues.   They wreathed and hissed
        for the sake
Of her caresses.   One of enormous size in haste
Did spring and coil around her waist.

The father of rattlers of prodigious size
With three score rattles and button on its tail
Coiled at her feet and rattled ready to assail
The first creature that showed disrespect.   Her eyes
It looked straight into with charming powers almost
        human,
Though charming invariably is done by woman.

This was their morning salutation; when finished,
Took their departure tandem—usually led
By this great rattler. How wonderful! instead
Of coming forth to do harm, they wished
To show us, for their own sake,
That Satan is not always in the snake.

In the corner of the field there is a clear, deep pool,
Fed by a large spring near its center;
Within its depths were strange species of fish, not
     known to enter
Other waters. When Winter began to rule
O'er the land, flocks of wild fowl
Found comfort here, like a monk in his cowl.

She approached the bank and tapped on a stump:
Presently with fish the surface was covered
Many with mouth open, tail and fins quivering,
     hovered
Before her. Some in their zeal did jump
Out on the bank, to receive food from her hand.
Such manœuvres would nonplus the champion angler
     of the land.

Those she desired for food were placed on a string—
     the chickens!
Many nice ones were left behind. How anxious
They were to be strung—never dreaming that a fate
     as worse
Would befal them as falls on yellow-legged chickens
Whenever the city minister goes in the country to
     dine,
How destructive to poultry is the divine!

Of her winter residence we'll take cognizance,
'Twas a large walnut tree, in whose hollow trunk
There was an entrance at the bottom. Its roots drunk
From the water of the brook. Its branches, immense
In length, were annually laden with nuts,
The greater portion squirrels carried to their lofty
     huts.

In gaining admittance a person was compelled
To get down on all fours—on his hands and knees—
And kick his way through by degrees,
If partly out doors he would be held
Impossibility he might try in vain to wheedle
Like a camel in passing through the eye of a needle.

On entering this tree we crawled in
As creeps a burglar through the window
Of his victim's dwelling, or a boy neath the canvas
        of a show.
In the mysterious hereafter we should not be sur-
        prised
To behold these offenders crawling up into the skies.

When getting within we were astonished :
Instead of a mere hollow, as in other trees,
We beheld a small room with articles of ease
And luxury.   The round walls were finished
Off with choice walnut, grained of late.
Of course the wood was in its natural state.

A second story there was, to which she ascended
By pegs driven in the wall.   Honest Abe
Used to do the same.   Immortal Lincoln, who did
        save
Our nation, once occupied a sphere intended,
Only for the beggar.   Not till after the human voice
        is no longer heard
Will wonderful men cease to come forward.

In this room were stored her valuables,
Consisting of a chest of gold, a box of silver-ware—
Its antique design made us in wonder stare—
Where she obtained it 'tis impossible to tell.
The most beautiful was a vase
Which she kept separate in a morocco case.

She was no votary of fashion.   Her unavaricious
Purse craved not wealth.   Her angelic face
Was never clouded for want of pin-money—the acc,

In a girl's deck of happiness. Our daughters must
Be educated and shielded from every lust—
But the many dollars they cost us !

On the wall hung her mother's portrait
In a simple frame. Bright was the escutcheon
Of a grandsire who at Fort Mackinaw run,
His race—the same did many comrades ; an awful fate
Was theirs—victims of an Indian massacre
To which Wyoming or Deerfield would compare.

Her trumpery was cast into a scuttle or loft,
Like the refuse of our erring race in large cities,
That cannot get into the basement. 'Tis a pity
That in New York they should live in rooms oft
Looked up to by the wealthy pious class, who fret
'Tis nearer heaven than they can get.

There was a single window, an elliptic knot-hole
About breast-high ; through it in the night
Flitted in and out an owl. During daylight
A swarm of bees made their egress and ingress. The
     soul
Of industry was their example, and none
Of that large swarm were drones.

They made honey in a huge tortoise-shell,
The remains of her amphibious pet,
Which she killed and ate after having let
It fatten for several weeks. In the city sells
At high price plate of turtle-soup, hind-legs of frogs,
Delicacies as indecorous as a son of Erin just from
     the bogs.

In the loft, rather in a hollow limb,
There dwelt an owl that most the night through
Perched on the topmost limb, dismally whooed.
At night in this forest, by the starlight dim,
To hear the plaintive notes of this owl
'Twould almost frighten a hermit from his cowl.

THE BROKEN DEMIJOHN.

Throughout a midwinter day a gale had blown,
Which at dusk sank into a desolate moan ;
  leaped high in the street were great drifts of snow ;
  he moon shone cold on a colder world below.

Almost high as the moon a building appeared to rise,
Whose massive form by moonlight seemed as a
        pillar to the skies;
Here and there from its numerous windows, small
        and narrow,
Through tattered curtains, the rays of candles dimly
        glowed.

This was a Rookery.   From basement to garret
Humanity of every description had come to share it.
Of Virtue, of Temperance, of a Godly life, none did
        dream,—
A depraved swarm were they where vice reigned
        supreme.

Up 'neath the roof, through which the moonbeams
        fell,
A family, one of the most wretched and depraved,
        did dwell.
From the oldest to the youngest, since the mother
        was gone,
Had shared with the father of his demijohn.

Walter, the eldest of fourteen, with sin well weighted
Like his sire, had many a time been intoxicated.
To make himself more wicked and vulgarly rude,
Blasphemed like a middy; both smoked and chewed.

He sold papers, blacked boots, did odd chores,
And was ever ready to quarrel with his neighbors.
From one source or another he managed to earn a
        sum
That kept himself well supplied in tobacco and rum.

" Walter, my boy," said old " wicked Ike " Flea-
.hopper,
" The jug is empty, get it filled. Here 're few
coppers.
You had better fetch a loaf or two of old Tobas's
stale bread,
For these brats are howling like wolves to be fed."

On lighting his pipe Walter took up the old familiar
jug,
And in the hallway gave it a sort of an affectionate
hug ;
But in this embrace no affection did he express,
'Twas the cold that made him clasp it to his breast.

Rapidly he descended several flights of rickety stairs,
And paused just out of doors in the keen biting air.
Here he swung his benumbed hands to and fro.
At Jack Frost's edict his blood must soon cease to
flow.

As he started on " O Walter, wait," called Tinty
Lookinbill
In a tremulous voice, for she was quite ill,
" I have got to go begging. Ma wants some beer,
'Tis awfully cold. I shall freeze. O, dear ! "

" Tint, if you don't hustle along I'll break your
back ! "
Shouted her mother, coming forward as if to do the
act.
" You aren't good for nothing, you lazy little hag,
Only to eat and sleep. Get along there and beg ! "

The bright, twinkling stars cast their immaculate
smile
Upon this innocent waif—poor Tinty—misfortune's
child.
In His loving care the cold did her no harm
As she passed along the snowy street, soliciting alms,

The street was deserted save by a lone wayfarer,
Whom Tinty accosted, and he listened to the tale of
      hers.
" In the name of the Lord, my good little child,
I give you this " (a piece of silver).   He passed on
      with a smile.

Finished was Tinty's unpleasant task,
She entered a dive, filled was her flask ;
Homeward she sped as if on the wings of the wind
      bent,
In front the door she fell and broke the flask in
      fragments.

The broken wheel at the cistern, the pitcher at the
      fountain,
Was naught when compared to Tinty's grief moun-
      tain.
" Lord (I learned this word of the kind stranger),
Mother will beat me terribly—my life is in danger."

She sat in a nook between the building and a great
      drift
Sobbing bitterly.   And her face heavenward she did
      lift,
The great salt tears froze on her wan sunken cheeks,
And to her grief only listened the winds bitterly
      bleak.

" Lord," she said at length-for the second time,
" Could I but go to the stars that brightly shine,
Go anywhere just to get out of mother's way ;
She scolds harder and beats me worse every day.

" She says I am awfully wicked but never told me
      why,
And often wishes me dead.   I fear to die,
For mother says there is beyond the grave another
      world
In which shall burn forever all bad little girls.

"I were cold when I sat down.   My ! how warm 'tis
    getting.
In a nice room before a bright fire I am sitting;
I hear sweet music; somebody too is singing;
I see bright flowers; flowers everywhere are springing."

Reclining on the drift and unconscious is poor little
    Tinty,
Gazing at the stars with eyes wide open, that are
    somewhat squinty.
At this season Angels would take her up to their
    bourn,
Had not the Lord a noble mission for her to perform.

On the other side the drift paused Walter Fleahop-
    per,
Endeavoring to remove the demijohn's stopper,
"Confound my luck," he exclaimed, 'twas always ill,
Just wait till I get home, then I'll drink my fill."

Walter being a strong, active lad, cleared the drift
    with a bound.
Half-covered with snow, Tinty's unconscious form he
    found.
"By George," said he, "this must be Tom, the shiner,
He was half-sick, and I told him not to go out till it
    got finer."

He cleared away the snow as best as he could,
And recognized Tinty by her shawl and hood.
"My God!" he moaned, "tis Tinty, my Tinty Look-
    inbill,
O dear ! she is dead, for she lies so still.
I will go after her mother, the wretch has murdered
    her child,"
Exclaimed Walter stamping the snow frantically wild.
Hark from the bundle of rags there comes a faint
    sigh;
He sees her smile, with joy he is ready to cry.

With snow he clapped her upper limbs,
And wrapped his coat around her form so slim.
He attempted to carry her; it was a heavy task.
" Walter," she said faintly, " I have broken the flask.'.

" Well, Tinty, since you are safe and the beer is
        gone,
On the door-step I will smash father's demijohn,
Then he will have cause to growl at me too,
The same, I am sure, as your mother will at you."

" Walter, I wish you had let me slept on in the snow,
Soon I would never more have felt mother's hard
        blows.
There she stands, more tipsy than ever, in the door-
        way,
On learning what I have done what will she say?"

" Tint," called the mother, " You indolent jade,
You have been out playing, for you always played.
Instead of trying to beat a little sense into you,
I will send you out to beg another flask or two."

"Madam," interrupted Walter, coming boldly
        forward.
" I have something to say, so let me be heard :
Tinty broke the flask, and as for beer,
You will have to beg it yourself, I fear."

" Broke the flask ! you scamp, none of your lies.
You cannot draw the wool over my eyes,
You deserve to have every hair pulled out of your
        head ;
You tell the worst falsehoods that ever was said."

" Mother, it is a fact," said Tinty, in a husky tone,
" I slipped, and the flask broke upon a stone ;
It made me feel dreadfully bad, and I
Sat down in the snow to take a long cry,"

" It is a very fine yarn that you tell.
I shall start in and thrash both of you well.
You worthless scamp, I mean you, Walter Fleahopper,
You aren't worth a half-penny copper."

From her blear eyes rage flashed.
Like a mortal fury, she at Walter dashed
With upraised hands, clawing at the air—
She meant to seize him by the hair.

Walter with his fists kept her at bay,
She began to scream, and screamed away
Till almost every inmate came out,
Wondering what on earth the trouble was about.

" The scamp started in to thrash me," said Madam
    Lookinbill
To the crowd that in amazement stood still.
" He has learned Tint to lie like Ananias,
And to talk in a way that's very impious."

" Well, I swan," yawned indolent Ike Fleahopper,
For a boy to try to whip a woman 'tisn't quite proper,
But let the remembrance of this row from our minds
    sink,
If there be ill-feelings let's drown them in a good
    drink."

" That's right," said a score with hankering mouths
    of water,
Eager for a draught as to taste forbidden fruit was
    earth's first daughter.
" For patching up trouble there's nothing like a glass
    of grog,
Come, let the jug pass, as we're all agog."

" Now, pards," began Walter, " a broken bottle caused
    this trouble ;
I shall break the demijohn, which may make it double.

As the madam at Tinty has up her dudgeon,
Father can pitch into me with the same bludgeon."

He raised the demijohn ; above his head it went ;
Next moment at his feet 'twas dashed in fragments.
From the dazed crowd there came a groan,
As if life itself was at once to be overthrown.

The madam was first to recover, and shouted, " the
      scamp is crazy ! "
Ike Fleahopper you would half kill him, if you
      weren't so lazy.
The wasting of so much rum, what a pity !
'Tis the worst loss that ever happened in this city."

For possession of the spot where the demijohn broke
      there was a scrabble,
As if seeking safety from a fire by some patent fire
      escape, and the babel
We dare say, was never equaled since that time, long
      gone by,
When vainglorious man by a tower found he couldn't
      reach the sky.

Few of the fortunate got down on all fours and pressed
      their mouths to the spot,
Smacked their lips as if tasting ice when it is very hot;
The remainder, having looked on with jealous stare,
As we do on a Saturday eve at the fortunate one in
      the barber's chair.

While this unique scene ensued
We find Walter in a meditative mood,
Conning whether his pipe to break also ;
And his package of Durham into the gutter throw.

" It is," he said at length " far the better way."
Against the wall he broke his pipe of clay,
He gave the package of Durham a vigorous toss
Out into the street, and it fell almost across.

Close to where it dropped an old toper stood,
Who, on picking it up, exclaimed; " Ah, this wind
    blows me good,
See, it has wafted from somewhere this prize ;
Perhaps it came from where Dick Tripeborrow's ghost
    lies."

Walter yet strove against the wiles of Satan hard,
And scattered broadcast a pack of new cards ;
But it grieved him sorely on giving away his pocket
    pistol,
One that a chum of his had brought from Bristol.

" God help me," said he, " from all vice to abstain.
Let a Christian life be my sole aim.
To lead this sort of life years ago, I promised mother,
But failed to keep my promise, somehow or other. "

By this time Ike Fleahopper began to realize the loss
His anticipated exhilaration proved dross.
He started upstairs with a shapeless bundle of wicker,
Cursing and bemoaning the loss of his liquor.

Madam Lookinbill, who, by the way,
As usual, gave her tongue full sway.
On Walter and Tinty she belched forth a vituperative
    stream.
All were shocked at the manner she blasphemed.

Even the most case-hardened thrust their fingers in
    their ears,
That they might not her vituperation hear,
This sound-excluding act, we believe, was resorted to
    long ago
When sang the Siren to those aboard the Argo.

Then she grasped woman's ever-ready weapon—the
    broom,
Few blows with it left her in full possession of the
    room.

Among those who sought safety were Tinty and
    Walter.
With dire threats she tried to stop her child, but she
    failed to halt her.

For present we will leave the madam to herself,
To sulk out her wrath, for she was a morose elf,
We will however ascend into the top story, where
    the Fleahoppers reside
Where everything bespeaks that Comfort hath long
    since died.

There was a single apartment of about twelve by
    fourteen,
Lighted by a single window in the ceiling low and
    mean;
The walls at any moment seemed ready to collapse,
The poverty they encompassed made them appear
    so—perhaps.

The door so shrunken, hardly the casement it im-
    pinges,
Is ready, undoubtedly, from starvation, to drop off its
    hinges,
At one time there must have been a latch,
Which hath gone with these chickens we count on—
    yet unhatched.

A candle stuck with its own wax upon a small table,
Emits feeble rays, and in the gloom sable,
Mammon might behold such a pity-inspiring plight,
So to confer for his favors equally on all—which is
    ever right.

In the small broken stove there's no fire; not an em-
    ber
Glows cheerfully on this eve, late in December.
Round the cold hearth huddle six little Fleahoppers
    to shiver
And cry with cold, derided by Jack Frost, their mis-
    ery giver.

In rags they are, and, if out in a gale,
They might, as a kite, through the air sail
Onward and upward, perchance till reaching the
 realm of splendor,
And they receive in exchange a white robe from some
 rag-vendor.

The cupboard is empty. The last crust was devoured
As darkness o'er the great, splendid, yet wretched, city
 lowered.
Over this morsel they quarreled and fought,
In Lord Chesterfield's polite ways they never were
 taught.

Soon as the improvident father came indoors,
For something to eat, they set up howls by scores,
"Shut up," he growled, "of only your own wants
 you think,
Your hunger is nothing to my thirst for a drink.

After a while he placed the wicker-work between
 his knees,
And a single drop from it he tried to squeeze.
His work was about as difficult as for a beadle
Or a camel to pass through the eye of a needle.

Wrong side out he made several attempts to turn it,
He cast it in the stove and applied a match to burn
 it,
"O good," exclaimed the little Fleahoppers, "we are
 to have a fire,"
"No, you won't, you little brats," growled the sire.

He took it out and flung it in the furtherest corner.
Over the fate of their igneous friend each was a
 mourner.
To hush their cries, he began beating them, the carnate fiend,
But he had just commenced, as Walter and Tinty
 came upon the scene.

" There ! that will do, that's enough," exclaimed Wal-
    ter, petulantly.
" Remember this is a game in which I can also play,
And father, depend on it, if there's no other resource,
I shall have to restrain you by force."

" Yes, that is what it has come to, eh? You are put-
    ting on too many frills,
Breaking my jug, and trying to knock out Madam
    Lookinbill.
What mean you in bringing here that little minx ?
(Pointing out Tinty). She is the cause of it all
    methinks."

" This is to be her home till such a day,
Till her mother learns of a better way.
To defend the glorious cause in which mother did be-
    lieve,
By the grace of God I enlisted this very eve."

" I sort of expected this you; are just fool enough to
    be bilked
By those smooth tongued ladies in silk.
Who tell of such fine things in some remote hole,
Where a fellow can never have the comfort of his
    bowl.

" What care they for we poor, neglected creatures ?
Your mother used to attend their parties at the
    preacher's,
When, coming home she was completely upset,
Because she couldn't have fine pictures and costly
    carpets.

" Such things are intended only for the rich,
While we must not growl if our bed be the ditch,
For the labor of a dollar a day each meal of water
    and bread.
Was recently advocated by a very pious head.

" I don't intend to deliver a lecture, for I am no scholar,
But, depend on it, if you have the Almighty dollar
You can drive fast horses in the park,
And every other night with gay comrades be out on
    a lark.

" There's Tim Mug Kisser who, a few years ago kept a
    dive,
By the sins of fallen women and sots he thrived ;
He has become one of the most sanctimonious
    creatures.
T'other afternoon I saw him upon the street, arm-
    in-arm with Henry Ward Beecher.

"'Tis no use of striving against our predestined ills,
No more than can the water that's passed by turn the
    mill;
For our luck to change we may hope and wait,
Till Death, the great pacifier, seals our fate.

" In every land throughout every necessitude this evi-
    dent fact hath shown,
That all but few reap tares, instead of the grain sown
Ofttimes methinks God impartial in His decrees.
For multitudes are scourged while few go scot-free."

"Nay, father," replied Walter, "a men charmer is
    Fate,
Yield not to despondence, but learn to labor and to
    wait,
Put your trust in Him and on His mercy ever rely,
Soon these dark hours will all have passed by."

While the above conversation ensued,
Half-a-dozen voices clamored for food.
Walter had forgotten his errand to Tobas's,
He should have gone instead of indulging in his
    glasses.

Walter pacified them by setting forth on his errand,
Ike Fleahopper sought the remains of the demijohn
    he was as dry as a herrin ;
Again he tried to squeeze out a single drop,
The effort, as before, was fruitless, in despair he
    stopped.

As Walter returned what a sight met their eyes,
Nice warm bread, meat, cookies, and pies,
" Walter, what means this ? " asked the next oldest,
    " come explain,"
Replied he, " The Lord is with us again."

Presently a man came in with a scuttle of coal,
Which to Walter on credit was sold.
But not on his credit alone, as the dealer had heard
Walter express a belief in God's Word.

The stove was filled as it had not been for many days,
And when came first the warm, life-giving blaze,
All, save the father, were rapturously bent,
The flickering candle joined in the merriment.

Sat Ike, clapping a hand upon each knee,
His wrath was at a calefaction degree,
He muttered at intervals with mongrel sighs and
    yawns :
" What, am I to do ?   O my demijohn ! "
" Father," exclaimed Walter, " come and sup,"
And extended him tea in the cup,
The infuriated inebriate swept it away,
On the floor the cup in atoms did lay.

" 'Tis this you offer me, instead of something whole-
    some ?
O that I could oust you the same as Grover Cleve-
    land did Madam Folsom !
But we must live together—I enduring your ills
Like a Pacific Coaster when Hayes vetoed the
    Chinese Bill.

" **Not a penny** have I to satisfy my thirst within ;
I must drink cold water, you say.   'Tis as wind
To a half-starved wayfarer.   It seems you were born
To hedge in my path and all others with thorns.

" If I possessed the bill of a snipe,
.I might satisfy this thirst from a wine pipe,
Which has the bung out to give it vent,
That it may, like a lawyer's wits, sparkle, foment.

" I am as a wood-cock pecking a hole in an iron lamp-
      post,
Or blood-suckers, numerous as a host,
From a bell buoy trying to extract a drop of ichor.
My very soul shrieks for want of liquor.

" You, as Luther, have wrought a reformation,
And in departing from Satan's station
It would not have been surprising at all
If you did, Luther-like, cast an ink-stand at the
      devil on the wall.

" In order to accoy this longing woe
Let me have a pipe of tobacco.
You may object, declaring smoke and rum are twins
That entice the young to their palace of sin."

" Father, I am very glad to say, the truth is
I have neither pipe nor tobacco ; no ruth is,
I know, stamped upon your face
Because I cast these seducers to waste."

" He has gone crazy, yea, I swear :
He destroyed his pipe, tobacco, and my demijohn ;
'Tis impossible to live with him in peace,
For my own safety I shall call in the police."

He rose up. Walter confronted him at the door,
And admonished him such intentions to give o'er.
'Twas exhaustion that made him obey at length,—
He exhausted on Walter his feeble strength.

" Father, you must take a pledge—
The same as you took long ago—bekedge
The candle is almost consumed,
Make haste, already gathers the gloom.

" You must swear by the Bible," " Why 'tis gone.
Replied Ike Fleahopper, "long ago I put it in pawn.
On it the broker gave me six bits.
'Twas long ago—uncertainty o'er my recollection
        flits."

Replied Walter, " If it is really gone
You must swear by the broken demijohn."
The demijohn was brought forth,
And on it Ike Fleahopper took an oath.

Soon as the oath was taken
There came a cry at the door,
Intending the very deaf to awaken ;
Tinty trembled ; it was her mother.

" Why, my good lady, please walk in,"
Said Walter on admitting her. " We have been
        talking
On temperance. In time you appeared on the edge,
And I ask you to take a pledge."

" Yes, madam, do," Ike Fleahopper interceded,
" We are sinful, 'tis time we were weeded."
" Why, Ike, do you really mean it ?
My intemperate appetite, must I wean it ? "

She also took an oath on the demijohn,
And what rejoicing there was ! Little **Tinty**
Rushed in her mother's arms. Fears of her was gone
And tears of joy fell from those eyes squinty.

Ike Fleahopper embraced each of his children,
And then threw arms about the madam's neck.
To the lookers-on this was all bewildering,
To affection they had grown up in neglect.

" O, madam ! " exclaimed Ike, half laughing and half
    crying,
" I want you to be a mother to my motherless off-
    spring ;
Replied the madam, her blear eyes a-drying,
" O, Ike, I want you to be my lord—my king."

Walter, not being at all backward,
Approached Tinty in mood joyous,
" What our parent has said you've heard."
Replied she, " let about the same apply to us."

Ike Fleahopper and Madam Lookinbill soon got
    married,
Walter and Tinty also wed, after having ten years
    in single blessedness tarried.
At present they live, if this story be true,
In a brown-stone mansion on Fifth Avenue.

LAST OF OUR RACE.

Where our cities and forests now stand
Interminable fields of ice will extend their forms
And jeer at furious storms
    That waft snows o'er the desolate land.
The ocean has shrunk, the waves
And tide are in their grave.

The sun has lost his potent heat,
Sends forth, as now in Polar regions, wan rays
That behest Night to yield not unto Day
    All is enrobed in a winding-sheet,
Gelid and hoar, extending through the tropics;
Warmth has consumed its oil and wick.

    'Mid the ice there's one family left,
Having gathered in a meagre store
Of food, and when no more
    Their supplies cease to be bereft,
They are from their place of refuge,
They come to confront starvation, grim and huge.

    Few hours roll on. A single soul
Has the whole world to his desolate self,
He crawls feebly upon a shelf
    To watch the sun reach his goal;
When the last glimmer leaves the leaden skies
He stares vacantly, with death-dimmed eyes.

MAN IS MEASURED BY HIS MIND.

Man is measured by his mind,
    But more frequently by his pocket,
When a wealthy one woman finds
    She places him on her marriage docket.

Man is measured by his mind,
    Very few, it seems, appreciate it;
Intellects of the most brilliant kind
    Oft on their heads the beggar's cap fit.

Man is measured by his mind;
    With empty heads and pockets full,
He can welcome at every hearth find,
    And his vulgar ideas seem never dull.

EXULTATION.

There's exultation in the mind
  Of an author, as he, with weary hand,
At the end of his manuscript that kind
  Word Finis appends. There's a difficulty he can
Hardly surmount—to behold several quires of fools
      cap
On which he is to work while others nap.

How is he to begin the first chapter,
  Or how shall he open a canto,
In the first place he's after?
  Make several unsuccessful attempts, and grow,
Ere long, weary of his theme, as the most successful
      do oft,
Whether surrounded with luxury or hard pressed by
      poverty up in the loft.

At length it is finished, not to grow indelible,
  That which he has traced on paper ;
An author is not at all infallible,
  He doesn't always like to acknowledge the caper
Of plagiarism. At all times 'tis as difficult to be
      original
As to discover tranquil waters upon the side of a hill.

SPARKLING WINE.

O, 'tis the sparkling wine
  That ever gives me relief ;
It makes each movement divine
  Crowns care with a laurel wreath.

It I love to laud,
  'Tis the water of life,
'Tis nectar of the gods,
  'Tis the nepenthes when care is rife.

Of it I'll long and deeply quaff
　　Despite what the temperate say;
While others mourn I'll laugh
　　All sorrow quickly away.

Fill the beaker to the brim
　　And let the froth run o'er,
'or there's much joy in
　　The sparkling invigorating nectar.

All hopes are built of air
　　Which doubt so oft undermines;
I shall ever mollify my care
　　In a glass of sparkling wine.

'Tis the sparkling wine
　　That I so fondly prize,
'Tis the obliterator of every design
　　When dismay pours down from the skies.

Then fill the beaker to the brim
　　I'll drink the health of gods,
And in the merry din
　　Their virtues I'll laud.

THE END.

www.ingramcontent.com/pod-product-compliance
Lightning Source LLC
Chambersburg PA
CBHW020621030726
47497CB00007B/2355